The House in Smyrna

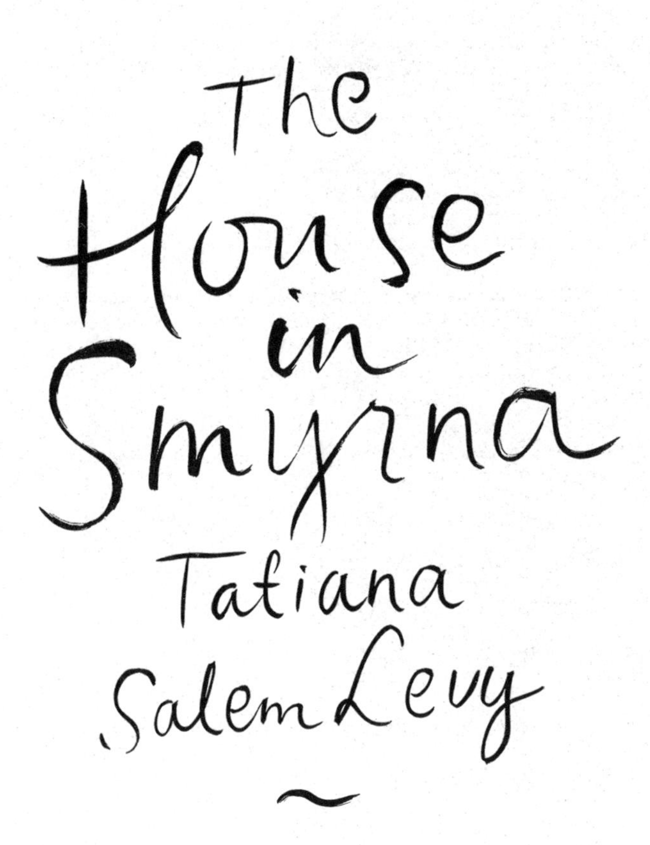

Translated by

Alison Entrekin

SCRIBE
Melbourne • London

Scribe Publications
18–20 Edward St, Brunswick, Victoria 3056, Australia
2 John St, Clerkenwell, London, WC1N 2ES, United Kingdom

Originally published in Portuguese as *A Chave de Casa* by Editora Record in 2007

First published in English by Scribe 2015

This work was published with the support of the Brazilian
Ministry of Culture/National Library Foundation

Obra publicada com o apoio do
Ministério da Cultura do Brasil/
Fundação Biblioteca Nacional

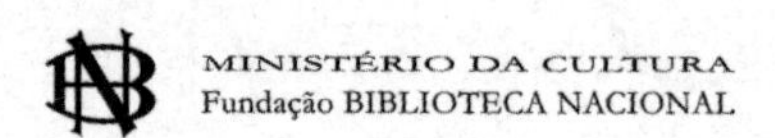

Typeset in Adobe Garmond 12/18.7 pt by the publishers
Printed and bound in China by 1010 Printing

National Library of Australia Cataloguing-in-Publication data

Levy, Tatiana Salem, 1979- author.

The House in Smyrna / Tatiana Salem Levy; Alison Entrekin, translator.

9781925106411 (Australian edition)
9781922247971 (UK edition)
9781925113600 (e-book)

Brazilian fiction–Translations into English.

Other Authors/Contributors: Entrekin, Alison, translator.

869.3

scribepublications.com.au
scribepublications.co.uk

To my sister, Dina, with love

~

They say that 'Time assuages' —
Time never did assuage —
An actual suffering strengthens
As Sinews do, with age —

Time is a Test of Trouble —
But not a Remedy —
If such it prove, it prove too
There was no Malady —

EMILY DICKINSON

~

I write with my hands tied. Here in the stationary solidity of my room, which I haven't left for the longest time. I write without being able to write, and I write for this. At any rate, I wouldn't know what to do with this body that has been unable to move ever since it came into the world. Because I was born old, in a wheelchair, with wizened legs, withered arms. I was born with the smell of damp earth, the stale gust of ancient times at my back. I am speaking of a weight that bears down on me, a weight that gives me stiff shoulders and a crooked neck, that holds my head in the same position for days on end, sometimes a month or two. A weight that isn't entirely mine, since I was born with it, as if every time I say 'me' I am actually saying 'us'. I always speak in the company of this age-old air that has accompanied me from the outset.

It paralyses me. A kind of burden. Weighty. More than that: it is brutal, cement-like, capable of arresting all movement, binding one joint to another, fusing my body's empty spaces. Not that I am sad. It's not a matter of being happy or not, but of a legacy I'd like to be rid of. Even if it means I have to take inordinate risks, even if it means giving up everything I've built thus far, everything I've believed to be my life. I've reached a point where I must change tack or be caught in Medusa's gaze and turned to stone, cast into the sea.

But words still evade me; the story isn't here yet. As long as my muscles remain heavy and static, meaning slips away. Perhaps, little by little, when I manage to take my first steps, when I am able to free myself of this burden, I'll be able to name things. And for this I write.

~

You can't imagine how relieved I feel. How long have you been lying on this bed, without moving? How long have I been asking you to get up? I don't know. I don't know the answer. It could be a week, a month, a year, or even a lifetime. At times I feel like a block of concrete; at others, a hazy cloud. I can't feel my shape, my contours. I want to move from here, but I still wonder if it's the right choice. *Don't lose heart. When you are setting out, there are no right or wrong choices, just choices. It's too early to judge.* But what if I make a mistake? What if I sink even deeper into this quagmire of imprecision and uncertainty? What guarantee do I have that I won't trip myself up? *There are no guarantees. I can only promise you one thing: take risks, and I will always be ready to give you my hand.*

~

To write this story, I must leave here and go on a journey to places I don't know, lands in which I have never set foot. A journey back, even though I've never left anywhere. I don't know if I'll be able to, if one day I'll leave my own room, but the urgency exists. My body can't bear the weight anymore, I've become a petrified cocoon. My face is haggard; the circles under my eyes are older than me. My cheeks sag, hearing the call of the earth. My teeth can barely chew. It is as if gravity has acted more intensely on me, tugging down twice as hard.

I have no idea what awaits me on this path I have chosen. Nor do I know if I'm doing the right thing — much less if there is any logic in the undertaking, an acceptable explanation for it. But I am looking for a purpose, a name, a body. And for this reason I'll make the journey back, to see if I haven't lost them somewhere — some place I have yet to know.

Without getting up, I take the little box from the nightstand. In it, amid dust, old tickets, coins, and earrings, lies the key that my grandfather gave me. Here, he said, this is the key to my old house in Turkey. I gave him a puzzled look. Now, lying here with the key in my hand, I still don't understand. What am I supposed to do with it? It's up to you, he said, as if it had nothing to do with him. People grow old and, afraid of death, pass on to others the things they should have done.

And now it is up to me to invent a destiny for this key, if I don't want to pass it on myself.

You hid it as best you could, avoided the word as long as possible. You promised me you wouldn't die of an illness. You promised me you wouldn't die. You promised yourself, clinging to the certainty you'd created, for my benefit as well as yours. I believed it; you wouldn't die. It meant we could live in peace: we created our world — our world without death — and in it we lived. It meant we didn't have to worry about things: we created our own certainties, and we lived without doubt. I joined you in your fantasy, went along with your game. We avoided the word together, and on we went.

You hid it as best you could, until the day you could no longer. At first, we simply turned our eyes from your bulging midriff, your swelling throat, but with time we were forced to see what we didn't want to. You had the belly of a pregnant woman, swollen lymph nodes on your neck, under your arms, in your groin. You tired easily. You felt queasy. You vomited blood. It was reality trying to defeat our fantasy: we couldn't live in our world anymore. The word we didn't want to say demanded to be pronounced, slowly and clearly. Our pact was crumbling.

You were sitting on the sofa looking defeated when I came over and whispered in your ear: don't worry. If we have to change worlds, we'll go together. It doesn't matter where — we'll make another pact and, if necessary, another, and then another and another and another. We'll make as many pacts as we need to, we'll change worlds as many times as we have to, but one thing is certain: my hands will always be clasped in yours.

I don't do anything but examine, touch, and gaze at the key. I know its details by heart, the exact size of its curves and handle, its weight, its spent colour. I doubt a key this size can open a door. Surely they've changed the lock by now, if not the door itself. It'd be foolish to believe it would be the same after so long. I'm sure even my grandfather knows this, but I also imagine that he must be curious to find out if what he left behind is still there. How strange, how bizarre it must be to leave your country, your language, and your family — to go somewhere completely new and, above all, uncertain.

He told me that the ship he travelled on was colossal, his first and only time on such a vessel. It was crammed with people, all with the same hope as him: to make better lives for themselves in a different country. He was the first of his siblings to arrive, with just two suitcases and a few contacts in Brazil. He was only twenty years old when he left Turkey. Some time later, his younger brother would join him. His twin sister would die of tuberculosis. His older brother would marry and remain in Smyrna. He would only see his mother again many years later, when, widowed, she decided to move to Brazil.

How many times have I heard this same story? The pain of never seeing his father and sister again, of never setting foot again in the land that was first his. Of only bringing his mother out in time to lose her. Of having seen so much poverty on the ship and in the land he'd left behind. How many times?

So what does he want now? For me to reclaim his history, retrieve his past? Why this key, this crazy mission?

~

The story isn't his alone. Life never belongs to just one person. If he gave you the key, it's because he believes it is part of your story. You know my father: he never does anything without a reason. He could have given the key to me or to one of my siblings, but he never did. I never did go to Turkey, and now I can't. I only heard his stories about coming to Brazil a few times. I'm not saying there's a destiny, a mission that only you can fulfil. As you know, few people are as sceptical as me. But I don't think we should turn down the things people offer us. How long have you been lying there in that bed? Maybe it's a good excuse to do something, to leave the incarceration of this room and visit a country you've never been to. Believe in this story that your grandfather is offering: go find his house and try to open the door. Retell his story; retell mine too. Take it as an opportunity to dig yourself out of the hole you are in, even if it leads nowhere, even if you don't find the house or the family that stayed behind. It doesn't matter. At least the scenery will be new — although it is so ancient.

She looked like a black bundle when she came to see her son off. Veil, dress, shoes, circles under her eyes, mouth — everything so black it was blue. She was dressed as if she were going to a funeral. His father looked more relaxed. He was wearing everyday clothes: a linen shirt buttoned all the way up and tucked into his pants. His red belt didn't match his brown shoes.

The expression on his face said that this was just a day like any other, although he knew in his heart it was different. It was as if the whole house knew it, but didn't say so: not only his parents and siblings, but also the ceiling, the walls, the unwashed dishes, the tidy living room (the orange cushions in their exact places on the sofa — one on each seat), the still-dark bedrooms. On this day everything and everyone bore an unspoken pain, an unspoken fear, an unspoken apprehension. The silence weighed heavily, begging the one who was leaving to please stay. They stood in a line in order of height: first his little brother; then his twin sister; then his older brother; then his father, the tallest of them all; and, finally, breaking the order, his mother. The door was still closed and the house was dark — there was just the light from the lamp and a subtle yellow glow coming in through the kitchen window. They must have been standing there waiting for him for a few minutes. They didn't look at one another or speak. They stood there stiffly, staring straight ahead at the living-room wall.

When he walked into the room from his bedroom, he wasn't surprised to see his family by the door, and knew that it was time. He had a suitcase in each hand and an overcoat on his right arm. He looked around attentively, as if he wanted to record in memory the whole composition of the house, the position of every object. He was afraid of forgetting. After all, he didn't really want to leave, but he needed to try a new life somewhere he could flourish. There was also the army: if he didn't leave Turkey, he'd have to serve, like his older brother. So he was bound for Brazil, where he had cousins and friends. Come, things are good here, there are lots of ways to make a decent living, they all said. Come, they need able-bodied young people like you.

Yes, wait for me; I'm coming.

I'm going to try my luck in Brazil, he told his parents. His mother looked mortified. From that moment on, she didn't speak another word to her son, or to her husband, as if he were to blame. She barely ate, barely slept. But it didn't stop him. He knew his mother and hadn't expected a milder reaction. And here he was now, suitcases in hand, ready to say goodbye.

He approached his little brother and, setting down his suitcases, lifted him into the air. The words he spoke to him were sweet, as an older brother's words should be. With his sister it was no different, except the tears on her face made him cry too. But he couldn't break down and give in to the pain or he wouldn't be able to continue. Tears were part of the choice. Then he hugged his older brother and it was his turn to hear some advice. His father gave him some too, but in a stricter tone of voice. He told him to be good; to resist the sins of the flesh and drink; to work hard, like a good member of the family; and, above all, to remember to write.

Last of all, the moment everyone feared. His mother was barely visible, blackened as she was by her mourning before the fact. His heart was filled with guilt, and he would carry it with him for the rest of the voyage, for the rest of his life. She was holding a package, supplies for the journey. When he turned to her, she held it out. And that was all. She didn't look at him, open her mouth, or make a gesture. As if to say: Take this and go, I don't want to prolong this moment. He understood. In silence, he took the package and opened the door. He could no longer look back, his body urging him forward. He left, behind him the still-open door, the still-silent house.

His mother placed her hand on the knob, gently closed the door, and turned the key in the lock. The moment was disconcerting. Everyone was waiting for her reaction, certain they'd find an expression of suffering on her face. But she was suddenly gripped by a kind of hesitant certainty. Instead of crying, she smiled. Maybe we'll see him again one day!

Nothing distresses me as much as saying goodbye to someone: *tchau*, farewell, *au revoir*, see you soon, see you never again. When I was little, when I could barely put a name to what I felt, you would leave every morning. As most people do, early in the morning, after breakfast. I knew you'd come back in the evening — but what if you didn't? Every morning, the same pain, the same tears: please don't go, don't leave me alone, stay with me, spend the day with me, come to school with me, go to the park with me, watch TV with me, read comics with me, have lunch with me. I have to go, you'd say, but I'll be back this evening. Don't worry, everything's fine. You came back, you always came back, you kept your word, but the next morning the pain was the same: there I'd be, at the door, blocking your way. I didn't want you to leave, sensing that something bad was going to happen. *I was just going to work. I wasn't going to abandon you. Where did you get this fear of separation? Why this pain before the fact? I didn't know how to react in the face of your desperate, excessive tears, your crying for no reason.* With time, I understood that you really did have to go, but I never stopped being afraid. I just learned to control myself. Certain kinds of behaviour were no longer befitting of my age. On the inside, I felt exactly the same. When you left, I'd go into my room and cry quietly, alone. Soon I just couldn't shut my eyes, or I'd start imagining tragedy after tragedy. So I'd turn the music up full volume and dance. I'd dance and dance and dance until I was certain the fear had gone.

I remember it so well: you were carrying some books under your arm, a light-coloured leather briefcase in your hand. We passed in the corridor on the sixth floor, looked each other in the eye, and glanced away sheepishly. But we were already captives, prisoners of what was to come. I don't know if you looked over your shoulder after we left the same horizon. A tingling sensation washed over me and I only kept walking because my body was carrying me, but the truth is that I was paralysed, gripped by a feeling that, no matter how hard I try, I can't name.

It was a while before we ran into each other again. I don't know exactly how long, but at any rate not long enough for the tingling to leave my body — that itch that you only feel a few times in life, that takes you by surprise but always gives you the impression that it was lurking nearby.

On the ground floor, heading for the bus stop, I was light on my feet, like a child dancing to nursery rhymes. I hadn't felt so airy in a long time. I didn't need anything else: I didn't need to know who you were, what you did, where you were from, if you were in a relationship. I had your gaze trailing through mine before I even knew your name, and that was enough.

I was born in exile: in Portugal, the country my family had been forced to leave centuries earlier because they were Jews. In Portugal, which granted my parents asylum when they were expelled from Brazil because they were communists. We had returned to where we started, we had come full circle: from Portugal to Turkey, from Turkey to Brazil, from Brazil back to Portugal. Wouldn't it have been less arduous, less bitter, if we hadn't been forced to make such a long journey? Why did we have to leave somewhere if we were only to return to it?

I was born in exile, outside my own country, on a cold, grey winter's day. Two hours of contractions without result, because I still hadn't turned and the anaesthetist wasn't there. My mother suffered in giving birth to me. And when I came into the world, she couldn't hold me in her arms because she'd been given a general anaesthetic. Worse: when she woke up, she realised they'd cut her open, up and down. She would forever bear the scar of my birth, a straight line, in relief, from the space between her breasts down to her pubis.

I was born in exile, and that's why I am the way I am, without a homeland, without a name. That is why I am solid, unpolished, still rough. I was born away from myself, away from my land — but, when it comes down to it, who am I? What land is mine?

~

There you go again, narrating through the prism of pain. That isn't what I told you. Exile isn't necessarily full of suffering. In our case it wasn't. I worked as a correspondent for a magazine in Brazil. Your father remained in the party. We were in Portugal, eating well, speaking our own language, meeting people, working, having fun. Your grandparents came to visit us; lots of people came to stay. We were always travelling: Paris, Florence, Madrid, Athens, Kiev. Yes, it is true, sometimes the uncertainty of our future weighed heavily: would we ever go home? But deep down we knew things would change in Brazil — we just didn't know when. No, dear girl, things weren't the way you describe them. When you were born, it wasn't cold or grey. I didn't suffer in giving birth to you. They didn't give me an anaesthetic; nor do I have a scar. I gave birth to you naturally. I held you immediately. You were loved and wanted, the result of a painless exile. When amnesty was declared, I didn't want to come back. You were very young and I would have preferred to stay on a few more years. But your father still believed in the party: he believed change was possible. So we returned, to make the revolution. There wasn't all this suffering that you speak of. On the contrary, there was much positivity and an enormous will to live.

~

I already had my ticket and only a few days to pack. I was going to Turkey first and then on to Portugal. Because it was summer, I didn't need to worry about cold-weather clothes. Nevertheless, packing is always a mixture of elation and worry. Great, I'm going to travel, I said to myself. Then I immediately started fretting that it would all go wrong. Then the elation of leaving came back. I spent the days packing and unpacking my suitcase, as my emotions swung back and forth. Sometimes I thought I might stay longer than planned and would stuff in all manner of clothes. Then I'd think I wouldn't even last five days, and out they'd come again.

I had never travelled like this before, with an objective to fulfil, but after listening to my grandfather and giving it some thought, I had decided to accept the challenge. At the very least I might find some meaning for my pain, and maybe even a way to free myself of it. I wanted to walk again, to find my way. And it struck me as logical that if I retraced, in reverse, the path my forebears had taken, I would be free to find my own.

The day I left, I had to get help to close my suitcase. Even though I'd rolled up my t-shirts and flattened my pants as much as possible, it was stuffed to bursting with clothes. It's always best to err on the side of excess. I sat on top while a friend helped me lock it. Are you going for good? he joked. You never know, I replied.

When the doctor came into the room, he was holding a jar with a weird, squishy object in it, almost as big as a melon. We stared at it, waiting for him to say something. He smiled, a smile that wavered between sarcasm and contentment, and announced: This is your spleen.

That thing? you said in surprise. And what makes you think I'd like to see it?

Because it's your spleen, he said, disappointed.

I couldn't take my eyes off the jar, staring with a mixture of disgust and fascination. I was looking at an organ. A sick organ. It was your spleen. And yet when I looked, you were still there, alive. You didn't need it to carry on. Look how big it was!

Normally a spleen is about twelve centimetres long. Yours was thirty.

Your eyes bulged. Really?

The doctor came closer with the jar, but you looked away. That's enough, you said, please don't insist.

He told us about the surgery and post-operative procedures. I couldn't take my eyes off the spleen. It looked soft and slimy.

A month earlier, the doctor had given you the news: you would need an operation. Your spleen was very swollen; the malignant cells were proliferating.

But how will I live without a spleen, doctor?

Well, anyone can live without it. It's a useless organ.

If it's useless, why do we have it? you asked like a curious little girl.

The doctor didn't answer. He just noted down the hospital and date of the operation in his planner. We left feeling cold.

I've never had an operation, you said. I'm afraid.

Relax, I said. Didn't you hear him? Everything indicates that it'll be simple, without any risks. As I spoke, I stared at your belly, an enormous ball. You'll feel a lot better afterwards.

I know, but I'm scared anyway, you said.

You'll have time to get used to the idea, to prepare yourself. But don't blow things out of proportion. Trust the doctor, he knows what he's doing. If he said you can live without your spleen, and that the operation is simple and for the best, then believe it.

When we got to the car, you were sweating. Do you want me to drive? I asked.

It was a long month. Every day we thought about it, talked about it. Fear was plastered across the walls of the flat. Every morning the same anxiety, wishing that time would pass quickly, and that time wouldn't pass at all.

What day is it today? you'd ask me first thing each morning.

Stop worrying so much, Mother. Relax, you'll be fine, you'll be fine, I'd say. And you'd answer like an echo: Yeah, I'll be fine.

In all honesty, it hadn't passed through my mind that the operation wouldn't go well. The doctor had been very optimistic and had explained how simple the procedure was, and I'd believed him. If it weren't for the fear stamped across your face, I wouldn't even have thought about it until the day you were admitted to hospital.

I dreamed every night of the scalpel cutting into me. They were going to take out a piece of my body, and I was afraid I wouldn't be able to live without it. I was afraid they might cut me in the wrong place, that they wouldn't find my spleen, that they'd cut out another organ, that they wouldn't be able to close me up again.

It was very early, still dark out, when we left the flat. You had to check in ahead of time so they could start you on medications and make sure you were fasting. The minute we set foot in the corridor, we were struck by the cold hospital smell. Your hand was sweaty, but anyone looking at you would have thought you were calm. Your sister and Dad arrived a short while later. First, two nurses came in and, after introducing themselves, put you on a drip with medications. We sat there chatting, trying to lighten the mood, to give the day some semblance of normality. Your sister talked about work, Dad talked about things in the news, and you and I listened more than we talked. An hour and a half later the doctor arrived, with the same smile he gave us every other time we met him: All up, the surgery shouldn't take more than an hour, two at the most. You barely took in what he was saying, as the sedative was already beginning to take effect. First, we're going to give you a general anaesthetic. Then we're going to open you up and remove your spleen. It's all very simple.

When you were wheeled into the operating theatre, lying on the stretcher, you were mumbling things that barely made sense, like someone talking in their sleep. I held your hand until we got to the door and I had to let go. It hurt to have to leave you on your own, but I continued trusting in the doctor's calm words. I went back to the room, where Dad and your sister were. We all wore serious expressions. Let's go downstairs and get something to eat, said Dad. We spent more than an hour in a restaurant on the same street as the hospital, talking about anything but you, while the doctor took out your spleen. I think we'd best get back, I said. They might have finished. When we got to the hospital, it was a while before we were given an update. Everything was going well, but the operation was taking a little longer than expected.

Almost an hour later, I felt my heart leap when the nurses brought you back. I stood quickly, needing to see you. You were lying on the stretcher with a sheet over you. You were awake, but still groggy from the anaesthesia.

Are you okay, Mother?

You grunted something I couldn't understand.

Ever since she left the theatre, said one of the nurses, she's been asking for someone by the name of Vivi. Are you Vivi?

No, I said, worried that you'd gone mad, that you'd forgotten my name. And I started repeating like an idiot: Mother, it's me, don't you recognise me? And you said: Vivi.

Who's Vivi? I asked, convinced by the nurse's certainty that Vivi was a person. You just kept repeating: vi-vi, vi-vi, vi-vi. Then suddenly I understood. You weren't calling for someone, you were announcing to yourself and the world: *Vivi!* I'm alive! It was only then that I realised the extent of your fear. When I let go of your hand and you were taken into the operating theatre, that was what you had felt. I hadn't understood a thing. I hadn't sensed your fear. It hadn't crossed my mind that something might go wrong. You were just having your spleen out. It was only when I realised that Vivi wasn't a person that I understood — for the first time — that your fear wasn't just any old fear of something unfamiliar: you were afraid of dying.

The first time we went out for a beer, I already knew what awaited me. We were in a bar somewhere in Botafogo. We didn't know each other very well, but I was already smitten. I couldn't think about anything but your body, your voice, the way you walked, gestured, dressed. You said you had a huge crush on me, that there was something about me. You said you hadn't felt this way about someone for a long time, as we drank beer after beer. I listened to every word and felt my body quake: with fear, desire, happiness. You spoke words of passion, and I believed them. But at the same time I gazed into your eyes and knew everything, discovered everything. I gazed into your eyes and understood that, even if you came to love me, we'd never love each other in the same way. I knew from the start that my love would always be stronger than yours and, as a result, I also knew the suffering that awaited me. It was our first date, and I was overjoyed to be sitting beside you. It was a gigantic feeling that barely fit inside my small body, although it came mixed with a kind of pain in anticipation, as if I were foreseeing our future and divining in your eyes all the happiness and all the sadness that were in store for me.

He was already on the ship when he felt a tightening in his chest, his stomach churning with anxiety: only he knew the real reason for his departure. You can always make a better life no matter where you are, but you can't run away. No, to run away you need to board a ship and sail many miles, especially if your reason is love, an impossibly big love, as his was. He was travelling third class and his bunk was small, among so many others. The air had smelled sour since the start of the voyage, and he thought it would be hard to bear the stench, the strangers, the screaming children, and the drunks, while carrying so much pain. Truth be told, he wasn't motivated to start a new life so far from his roots. What was more, he'd heard that the streets of Brazil were teeming with rats, cockroaches, and wild animals, rubbish scattered everywhere, and the air was so hot you could barely breathe. But it was where he had cousins, contacts, people who could help him. He couldn't stay in Smyrna.

An old man deposited his belongings on the bed next to his with a frown, as if to say he didn't feel like chatting. It's for the best, he thought, since he wasn't really in the mood to get to know other people either. He preferred to keep to himself, lying on his bed, thinking his own thoughts.

Rosa was her name. When her father had found out that she and one of his shop employees were exchanging glances, he hadn't hesitated to take drastic measures. Rosa was only allowed to leave the house in the company of her older brother, whose job it was to ensure their father's orders were obeyed. My grandfather was fired. Get out, go get a job somewhere else, preferably far from my establishment, my house, my neighbourhood, my country. He had been looking for another job for a year and it was only now that he was taking his former boss's advice. Only now, on the eve of Rosa's marriage to the young man her father had chosen for her.

In his suitcase were the few letters he had exchanged with her on the rare occasions that they had managed to be alone, even if only for a few quick seconds. When he'd heard of her engagement, he'd spent a few days locked in his room until he decided to leave for a distant country. Before departing for Brazil, he gave her one last letter full of sweet, tender words and swore that his love was eternal.

When I arrived in Istanbul, I was holding my Portuguese passport instead of my Brazilian one, thinking it would be less of a headache. There was a long queue in front of the federal police counter. Turks on one side, foreigners on the other. When it was my turn I heard: You need a visa.

What?

It's the law. Portuguese citizens need visas.

But I'm not Portuguese, I'm Brazilian. No, I'm not Brazilian, I'm Turkish. My grandfather is from here; my forefathers were all Turks. I am too. Don't I look Turkish? Look at my long nose, my small mouth, my olive eyes. I'm Turkish.

The officer sniffed. You need a visa.

I didn't bother to argue. I'd never convince him. I turned and headed for immigration. Peeved, indignant, and disappointed. I needed a visa to enter the country of my ancestors? They were born here, grew up here: didn't any of that matter? Ten euros and a stamp in my passport: *úç ay süreli müteaddit giri vizesidir. Çali ma hakki vermez.* I have a three-month tourist visa, but I can't work. I am definitely not Turkish.

You were already blind in one eye when the doctor said: There's nothing else I can do. If you can afford it, your best bet would be to try a hospital in the United States. Maybe there they can stop the disease from advancing.

We didn't hesitate. We packed our bags and in two days we had moved country.

The first time I rang your doorbell I knew I was signing a contract without an expiry date. If any kind of rescission were possible, it should have been established there, at that moment, before walking through your door. But how could I not walk through it? Why not walk through it? My body still wasn't paralysed, I wanted to walk; I wanted to see what had caught my attention on the corner, discover what was waiting for me on the other side of the road. In those early days, my passion manifested as hunger — for novelty, conversation, caresses, sex. I wanted to devour everything in front of me, everything that came from you. And that is what happened. I rang the doorbell, perspiring. My t-shirt clung to my torso, lightly outlining my breasts. When you opened the door, I couldn't disguise my desire to jump on you, right there in your front hall. You ran your hand across my face, taking your time behind my ear, my neck. You tidied my hair with one hand and held the back of my neck with the other. You were asking too much of me at that moment, requiring that I be patient. I let myself be led, containing my fury and desire to control. And therein lay my pleasure: in being surprised, in being guided somewhere unexpected. With each touch of yours, fingers, lip, nose, I felt my skin quickly unravelling, in contrast to the slowness of your movements. You stared at me — eyes, chin, breasts, stomach — as if you wanted to destabilise me, lift my feet off the ground. And you did. At that moment, I was already treading on air. My feet were no longer in contact with the earth. There was no doubt in your mind: I was already yours. And, as if wanting to show me that you knew it, you held me firmly, squeezed my arms, and pressed your mouth to mine, your tongue to mine. You ran your hand down my body. The further your fingers probed, the more vulnerable I felt. Your tongue found my breasts, one and then the other, and slid around my nipples, leaving them almost as wet as I was below, still waiting. Not for long, it is true, because I soon felt your hand under my skirt, my legs parting slightly, the invitation already made. And, as I was able to testify so many other times, few things excited me as much as your fingers pulling aside my knickers, leaving me exposed. To quickly cover me again with your fingers. Take me to bed, I said. You pretended not to hear. With both hands, you lifted up my skirt, yanked off my underwear, and then kneeled slowly. I remained standing while you implored something between my legs, in a language understood only by the two of you, my clitoris and your mouth.

On the walls of the room, just moss. The stench of a closed environment. Objects green with mould. Everything falling apart, old before its time. In the middle of the room lies my bed of rotting wood. I don't even know how it is still standing. In the middle of the bed lies my body. Dilacerated, covered in open wounds, purple and yellow spots, boils. Corroded by the ancestral nature of the room. Almost incapable of movement.

In the middle of my body sits the typewriter. Its keyboard almost entirely erased, its ink almost gone. My blood-caked hands type these words, one letter at a time.

~

I left the airport still indignant about needing a visa. Better to forget the whole thing quickly. The lack of recognition on the part of Turkish Immigration wouldn't change my relationship to the country in the slightest. Or maybe they were right and I wasn't Turkish after all. Maybe I had no reason to be there. I'd be a tourist like any other, I thought, wandering through mosques, boating on the Bosporus, eating lamb, visiting castles and museums, buying rugs, leather, and spices in the Grand Bazaar. I'd ask people in the street to take pictures of me and I'd say *cheese* at the right moment. I'd be the most foreign of tourists, awkwardly asking for information, laughing at things that weren't funny. I'd take guided tours and see the city from the top deck of a bus, paying attention to everything the guide said. I'd go to restaurants where there was belly dancing, women with gyrating hips. Then I'd return to Brazil and invite my friends over to see the photos. I'd tell everyone what a beautiful country it was, that I had never imagined it was so exuberant, with enormous palaces and mosques, overflowing with the wealth of times past. I'd tell everyone I'd never seen anything so different before, a mixture of Eastern and Western cultures. I'd tell everyone that most of the women wore headscarves or veils. That the men stopped working when they heard the call to prayer. I'd tell everyone that the city was a little dirty, but very safe — you didn't have to worry about going out with your camera hanging from your neck. I'd tell them all that they had to go, they had to visit Istanbul, it was worth it, really worth it, the most beautiful city I'd ever seen.

With the name of the hotel in hand, I turned down all taxi offers between the arrivals area and the airport exit and tried to find a cab myself. After walking a distance, I spotted a row of cars. There, I thought. I showed the piece of paper to a man, who, in turn, showed me to the car that would take me to my destination. I didn't need to do a thing. Both the man to whom I had handed the piece of paper and the taxi driver put my bags in the car.

The airport was far from the hotel, and after a while the silence started to bother me. Do you speak English? I asked the driver. A little, he replied with a thick accent. I sensed that the conversation wasn't going to go very far and didn't insist. To be honest, I didn't actually have anything to say. He was the one who asked if it was my first time in Turkey. You'll love it, it's a beautiful country, the people are friendly, very welcoming. After the praise, I couldn't help myself and said with conviction:

My grandfather is from here, from Smyrna.

From Smyrna? He didn't seem to believe me. As he drove, he glanced over his shoulder once, twice, three times to get a better look at me. Suddenly, as if stating the obvious, he proclaimed: Of course. You have a Turkish face: the olive skin, the long nose. I don't know how I didn't see it before. But… you don't speak Turkish, do you?

No, unfortunately. My grandfather didn't teach my mother his language.

After my revelation, he was even friendlier. We chatted all the way to the hotel. He told me I'd really like the city and, who knows, maybe I could return for a while to re-establish my roots? I slowly recovered the good mood that I'd lost in Immigration. Perhaps there were other things to do besides boat tours and visiting mosques and museums. The driver had already convinced me: I wouldn't be just another tourist. I had a Turkish face.

I laughed my head off when you said you loved it when a woman had her period. What do you mean *love* it? What exactly do you love? The smell? The colour?

The taste, you said.

I laughed and half-grimaced. No way.

Oh yes, you assured me, yes way.

I hesitated a few seconds, the time I needed to take in your reply. Okay then.

~

Last night I had a strange dream. A nightmare. I arrived at my grandfather's house in Turkey, a big, beautiful, very old house with ornate walls, like an embroidered dress. The salmon-coloured paint looked fresh. The door — of dark, chiselled wood, swirls within swirls — occupied almost half the wall. And the almost imperceptible lock, instead of being located on the right, next to the latch, was on the left, near one of the hinges. I plunged my hand into my bag, sure that the key was there, but to my surprise there wasn't one but many — a dozen perhaps. All enormous! Proportional to the door but not to the lock. I threw my bag to the ground and, in desperation, began to rummage among the keys for one that was the right shape and size. But the harder I looked, the more keys appeared, and in the end there must have been a hundred lying around me. I repeated to myself: It isn't possible. It has to be here. I know it's here.

Suddenly, I heard a loud creak. It was the door opening. A man of about my father's age appeared, inviting me in. It's here, come inside, come into your house. I was surprised. Why was this man speaking Portuguese? Come, he said again. When I entered, the house was full of people, young and old, and they all had something familiar about them. The men were wearing kippahs, and most — but not all — of the women had white scarves draped over their shoulders. They surrounded me, hugging me, welcoming me: This is your home, they said. The table was laden with bread, honey, apples, matzah, wine, boyos, cheese, bourekas, and almonds. Come, take a seat, we've made you some treats.

I wasn't hungry, but the smell was so inviting that I couldn't resist. I started with the cheese and the eggplant bourekas. But I soon realised that I was the only one eating; in fact, I was the only one sitting at the table. As I ate, they all just stood there watching me, as if I were a strange animal, an exotic jungle creature. I stopped chewing and looked for a face that I recognised. I was afraid. They all noticed and began to laugh. I raced to the door, wanting out, certain that I was in the wrong house. Then I heard a deep voice say: This is your family! I tried to open the door, but it was locked again and now I had no key at all. The laughter grew louder and louder, as I screamed: Where's the key?

I woke up drenched with sweat, lying in my bed, in my room, in my apartment.

~

Almost every day there are moments in which I do something and immediately afterwards think: That wasn't me. Silly, everyday things, like smiling, curling up on the sofa to read the newspaper, or holding a cup of coffee with both hands. Suddenly, mid-gesture, I get the feeling that it isn't me. When I start laughing and can't stop, for example, I'm sure it's you who's laughing. *It's true; we're very alike. I've had that feeling too and I'd look at you and think how alike we are.* But it's not just that, it's a weird feeling, an absolute certainty that it isn't me. It isn't always you. Sometimes it's Dad, sometimes Grandpa, sometimes it isn't any of you. Sometimes I sense that it's someone I've never met, but who speaks through me. As if my body weren't mine alone. I sense this multiplicity all the time, other people accompanying me. *But it's just a feeling; it isn't real. You are you, full stop. The rest, my dear, are just similarities that remind us of other people.* No, Mother, I won't reduce what I feel to such a simple word: similarity. I'm not saying that they are spirits, but the word 'similarity' doesn't exactly do it justice. I might not be able to convince you, but I know that when my back hunches over like a hook it isn't just me who is hunched over. I know, Mother, even if I can't find the right word, that my body is not mine alone.

In the beginning we didn't even see the light of day, shut away in the bedroom as if we'd spent our entire lives waiting for that moment. We forgot everything on the outside and spent days and nights in bed.

He learned of Rosa's death in a letter from his sister. He had already been in Rio de Janeiro for a few months, working with a cousin and making plans to open his own hardware shop. He missed his family and wrote them at least once a week. The letters from home were almost always the same. It seemed that nothing had changed after he left. His heart sped up every time he received an envelope from Turkey. He'd open it in a rush, anxious for news or a word of encouragement. His sister wrote about their father's work, their mother's health problems, and a few bits and pieces about their older brother, who was soon to be married. The youngest did nothing but talk about Brazil. He wanted to follow in his brother's footsteps, try his luck there. She, in turn, was waiting to see what would come of their father's search for a husband for her. *But I don't want to get married like that*, she wrote. *I want to marry for love. Won't Father ever understand? I don't want a husband chosen by him. I want to be able to choose one myself. Don't you agree with me, dear brother?*

His heart went out to her. He knew what she was talking about. *I'm afraid I'll go the same way as that girl Rosa. Remember Rosa, the daughter of your old boss at the shoe shop? Well, apparently she was in love with a young man of whom her father didn't approve. Afraid they might elope, he quickly arranged for her to marry. He sent for a lad from Istanbul, the son of a good family, childhood friends of his. She refused to accept his decision, and didn't want any man but the one she loved. But you know how things are done here. Rosa had no say in it. Do you know what she did?*

He froze. His heart was in his mouth, fear of the answer flooding through him. He couldn't continue reading the letter, but he couldn't not read it. *With a stone tied to her ankle, she threw herself into the well in the square. She killed herself, dear brother. They found her body floating there, her dress puffed out by the water. Can you imagine the scandal? The family refused to mourn her death, and now the community is using her as an example to convince young women to marry suitors chosen by their fathers. But shouldn't it be the opposite? Don't you agree that the whole story shows us the impossibility of a loveless marriage?*

He shook, feeling his stomach churn, his legs incapable of sustaining his body. He was filled with regret: he should never have come to Brazil — or he should have brought her with him.

~

Before leaving Brazil, I had never imagined it could be so hot here. I stopped at a café for a juice and analysed the map that the hotel receptionist had given me. Seen like that, on paper, Istanbul struck me as a city like any other. I looked for the street the hotel was on — which took a few minutes — and realised I wasn't far from the city centre. I just didn't know whether to go this way or that, right or left. I wanted to go to Eminönü, where the main mosques were. I wanted to start with the obvious and then allow myself to be carried away by the unknown. I paid for my juice and asked the waiter which way to go. His answer was friendly but no good to me, as it was in Turkish, even though he'd nodded when I asked if he spoke English. I ended up taking a taxi: The Blue Mosque, please.

It was impossible not to be awed. I had no regrets, no fear; the minute I set eyes on that immense, imposing structure, I was certain I'd made the right choice. Not only was it monumental in size, with its tall, thin spires (at the top of which I detected a fine layer of blue paint), but also it was delicate and earthly in its tiny details. I forgot everything around me: the heat, the unpleasant smell, the hordes of tourists and street vendors. I forgot the reason for my journey: the key, the door, my grandfather, the past. It was just me and the mosque, as in all great love stories. We were eternal for a few seconds: the mosque, staring at me in its nigh almightiness, and I, staring at the mosque in my patent fragility.

And that was how I adored it, how I admired it as I had never before admired a monument. I spent a long time walking around it, putting off the moment of entry for as long as possible. I saw a corridor with a row of taps and low stools. Halfway down it, two younger men and an elderly one were washing their feet, faces, and necks. I was so hot, and welcomed the idea of freshening up a little. I imitated them — sitting on a stool, I turned on a tap and wet the exposed parts of my body. The younger men looked at me and laughed and whispered. The elderly man stood and, before I knew what was happening, he was beside me, waving his hands, talking in a loud voice. I couldn't understand a word he was saying, but I understood that I shouldn't have been there, that I was doing something very wrong. I hurried out, red and embarrassed, and the young men laughed even more as the irate older man returned to his place and resumed his ritual. Only later did I discover that not only was the place sacred, but also that it was reserved exclusively for men, who had to purify themselves before entering the mosque to pray.

I walked away quickly and headed around to the main entrance. I climbed the stairs and found a rectangular paved area with a kind of miniature mosque in the middle of it. Behind it was an enormous wooden door, ornately carved, through which people came and went. Outside I saw lots of families — children, and women with scarves on their heads, others with veils, and one with a burqa, covered entirely in black, with only her eyes visible. I had already seen women like that in newspapers, on television, and in films. But seeing one in front of me, with everything hidden — her body, face, and hair concealed — was odd: I felt a great distance separating us, a deep gulf, and at the same time an understanding that is particular to women. That could be me, I thought, and wished I could uncover her. I wished I could see her. It wasn't mere curiosity — it was as if I needed to be near her, to touch her, to pull down the barrier between us. When she realised she was being observed, she got up, crossed the paved area, and sat where I couldn't see her, directly behind the central structure. I blushed again. It was the first time I had set foot in such a different world and I couldn't hide the fact that I wasn't a local. I was committing all kinds of faux pas that they wouldn't. I felt ashamed. I didn't want to be an outsider, but it seemed inevitable.

When I went to enter the mosque, a man approached me and gave me a scarf to cover my head and another for my legs. I also had to remove my shoes. I saw two young men talking, both with credentials hanging from their necks. One of them introduced himself and we chatted a little, and then he asked if I wanted him to accompany me during my visit. I accepted. I wanted the company of a local, and he seemed nice. I'm not a guide, he said. I work here in the mosque and I can tell you a few things about its history. Then he told me when, how, and why it was built, the meaning of some inscriptions, why it was called the Blue Mosque, as well as its real name. He showed me the direction of Mecca and how Muslims prayed. A boy walked past us wearing clothes that I imagined a prince might wear. He was dressed like that because he was going to be circumcised. But at that age? I asked. Yes, some do it when they're still babies, but most have it done between the ages of five and eight. It's a moment of great joy for them. I asked the boy if I could take his photo. He agreed and posed with a big smile on his face, clearly proud to be dressed in ceremonial attire.

The mosque was enormous and there was hardly anyone in it. I tactfully asked the man accompanying me if I could be alone for a while. I am not Muslim, or even religious, but something about the place gave me a feeling of peace, and I felt an urge to be alone — just me with my sadness, me with my happiness.

I was about to nod off in the silence when he approached me again to say that I had to leave. In a little while prayers would begin, and tourists weren't allowed inside while they were taking place. I left quickly, afraid of committing another gaffe. At the door, I returned my scarves and put my shoes back on. The young man was still there and said he wanted to show me one last thing. We crossed the paved area and he asked me to look carefully at the pillars to see if I noticed anything unusual. I said no, I couldn't see whatever it was that he wanted me to see. He pointed to several names written in Arabic, almost completely faded. Those are the names of the stonemasons, he said. Every time they finished a section of the mosque, they'd leave their signatures.

We exchanged a few more words and then he excused himself: I have to go. I must get ready for my obligations.

I left the mosque in a state of thrall. I strolled across the paved area without looking where I was going: my feet were there, but my mind was elsewhere. I was sitting on a bench when I heard a voice flood through the square, through the city. It seemed to come from nowhere, from somewhere distant, somewhere unknown. It was rasping, melancholic, a true lament. I felt like I'd heard it before, but I was also certain I hadn't. I saw people quicken their pace, hurry back and forth. It must be the call to prayer, I thought. The voice persisted, echoed, and continued to resonate even after the singing had stopped. It stopped and started again, finding a few people still in the street. I took out my camera, which also captured sound, and recorded it. I wanted to be able to hear it in the future, in other places, at other times. Again, the voice rested and then resumed the call. The square emptied almost completely: I didn't see the boys selling knickknacks, the kebab vendors, or even the birds. Just tourists like myself. The singing continued, stopping and starting about four more times, echoing unexpectedly in some archaic part of my body, with some memory of which I was not aware. The voice — a wail, a mournful cry — spread across the entire city until it ceased. Then Istanbul appeared to be dead, and I felt that something very old in me had begun to be reborn.

~

In the lift, on our way down, I asked: Why the hurry? I was really enjoying our conversation —

You said, It's you: the clothes you're wearing, your loose dress, your habit of not wearing a bra.

I made a face. What do you mean?

That's all there is to it. I can't help myself, you drive me crazy.

I smiled, a little disconcerted, and drew you into a kiss that lasted longer than the time it took to reach the ground floor.

We barely spoke in the car. You drove fast, ran red lights. Take it easy, I said. You turned and smiled. That was the nature of our desire: it would strike suddenly, and we'd have to go with it. I saw the way you were driving and understood that you couldn't have stayed at the dinner. I understood, because it happened to me too.

At home, you took off your shoes and went to get some whisky. In spite of your urgency, you made an effort to wait.

You served us and lit a cigarette. I'd like one too, I said. The cigarette was between my lips when you lit it. We sat there a while, drinking, smoking, looking at each other, smiling. Almost in silence, just the odd comment or two. Until you looked at me more lustfully, indicating with your eyes that the hour had arrived. I didn't say anything or ask anything. I just stood and slowly began to undress. I slid the straps of my dress over my shoulders, showing the top of my breasts. You fidgeted on the sofa. I smiled. I lowered the straps even further, revealing my breasts completely, and stepped out of the dress. Turn around, you said. Unable to see you, I felt all the danger of the world at my back. I knew you were staring at my arse, your favourite part of my body. It was a pretty obvious choice, but I was pleased nonetheless. I kept my back to you as I slipped off my knickers. My naked body, a bookcase of dark wood in front of me, and the certainty that you were staring at my arse. Turn around, you said again. We locked eyes: you, fully dressed, and I, completely naked. I couldn't have moved if I wanted to.

You stood and began to undress too. Your penis was hard, upright, and I liked seeing it like that, as if it were looking at me too. I liked gazing at your defined, almost hairless torso, your legs like those of a football player, your slightly muscular arms. You were still staring at me, with growing arousal, and your eyes touched me from across the room. We remained distant for a time, until our burning bodies could no longer bear the solitude, until they demanded the presence of hands, mouths, another burning body.

I tell (make up) this story about my ancestors, this story of immigration and its losses, this story about the key to the house in Smyrna, about my hope of returning to the place that my forebears came from, but you and I (just the two of us) know that the real reason for my paralysis is something else. I tell (make up) this story to justify my immobility, to give the world and, in a way, myself, an answer, but you and I (just the two of us) know the truth. I wasn't born like this. I wasn't born in a wheelchair; I wasn't born old. There is no gust of ancient times at my back. I became like this. I lost my movements one by one after you were gone. After I met death and it looked at me with its eyes of stone. It was death, your death, that slowly took away my movement, left me paralysed in this musty bed.

I don't want to be blamed for your paralysis. I am still holding my hand out to you, but I can't be an accessory to this madness of yours.

I didn't choose to depart, and you know it. Now it is up to you to manage your life. All I can do is offer you my hand, my words. Please understand: I am gone now, and the only way for me to live on is through you. If you give up, I will be dead. If you don't move, if you don't leave this dark room, I'll be stuck here too. Get up. Move. If not for yourself, for me. I'm not asking you to live without the dead, but to live with them. Listen to me just this once; make an effort. I'm not saying it's easy. All I ask is that you change the position of your lens, look at things from another angle. You haven't lost anything; you can never lose what is already yours. If you can understand the role of the dead in this life, you won't spend another minute in this bed. Don't give up, for if you do, you'll be giving up on me. Live on and I live on.

~

Istanbul is a city of doors. Not only the doors of mosques and palaces but also the ordinary ones — of people's houses, of small establishments — are intricately carved. Most are wooden, and you need time to appreciate them. On every corner I found new doors that I was drawn to for different reasons: the size of the lock, the complexity of the design, the colour of the wood, its weight, its smell. Sometimes I was surprised by the owners, who came out to ask if I was looking for something. No, I'd say, I'm just admiring your door. Some would smile, others would scowl, and yet others would tell me stories about their doors — how old they were, what this or that design represented, why they were made of such-and-such wood, why they were large or small. Sometimes they would explain these things to me in English, and I thanked them; other times in Turkish, and I thanked them too. What mattered was knowing that the object of my fascination had a meaning. And in that manner I readied myself for Smyrna: familiarising myself with doors so that I wouldn't have any unpleasant surprises when I came face to face with the one that awaited me.

I love to ride my bicycle in the middle of the night after making love. But it has to be one of those old-fashioned bikes with curved handlebars, basket in front. Full skirt, the wind uncovering my thighs. I like to ride fast, through almost-deserted streets, without stopping at red lights. I like to take wide avenues and then narrow streets and alleyways, lose myself along routes I don't know. My smile broad, without a trace of mystery, body still warm, arms and legs wobbly.

They found him lying facedown on the ground, a pool of dried vomit on one side and his sister's letter on the other. He hadn't shown up to work, and his cousin had sent his youngest to see if anything was wrong. The boy was seven and got a fright when he saw him lying there on the ground. He thought he was dead. He raced down the street crying, shouting that someone had killed his cousin. There was a great commotion, and neighbours from the whole street, busybodies, came to see the tragedy. Some people like to see bodies covered in blood, stabbed, run over, and then turn their faces away and say: How awful! They were already making up stories — that he must have brought some kind of illness from his country, that he'd had a heart attack — when his cousin, the hardware-shop owner, came and rolled his body over. He held his hand under his nostrils and saw that he was still breathing. He's not dead, he said, he's just unconscious. Few of those present were able to hide their disappointment. If he had merely passed out, what was all the fuss about? They went back about their business, except the cousin and a neighbour, who carried him over to the bed, tried to reanimate him, and gave him water. At first they wanted to take him to the hospital, but when he slowly regained his colour and senses, they thought it best to leave him where he was. He said he felt fine and didn't want to go anywhere. I'm sure it's no big deal, said his cousin. You know what the heat's like here ... Rest up today and you'll feel better tomorrow. He nodded, thinking that all he wanted was to be alone, in his bed, under the sheet. But he had to wait for his cousin to stop chatting, another hour or so, with the neighbour there too, laughing at his stories. They finally said goodbye. See you bright and early at work, okay?

The next day he didn't go to work, or the next, or the next. He didn't get out of bed for over a month. He barely spoke, just muttered sounds of discomfort. All he ate and drank were a few pieces of toast and cups of white coffee. He was growing weak and his relatives said it could only be *deskarinyo*, thinking of sending him back to Turkey on the next ship. Even those who had lived in Brazil for a while still mixed Portuguese with their mother tongue. That's why they said *deskarinyo*, which is their word for homesickness. They had already called the doctor, who said he was perfectly healthy: it must be in his head. What they didn't know was that he was shattered. That for him there were only nights, his heart a dark pit of sadness and guilt. He had lost his love, little Rosa, and felt both victim and culprit of the pain.

He spent a long month in bed, a truly endless night, thinking of Rosa's delicate hands, her fine lips, her long hair, her shy manner — that of a girl in love for the first time. She had been his first love too, and he told himself that she would be the only one, that he'd never again love another woman as he had loved her, as he still loved her. He thought about the soft body that he had never known, and everything he could have done but hadn't. And, when he thought that he should have stayed on in Smyrna and stood up to Rosa's father, ignoring customs and tradition, he felt his heart unravel further and anxiety flood his body. He felt so bad that all he could do was tell himself: I want to die. He even considered suicide, believing only death could alleviate his suffering. He also believed that, by dying, he would no longer be to blame; that if he came to the same end as his beloved, he'd be forgiven. But he didn't even have the strength to stand. His body and the bed were one, as he had once believed himself and Rosa to be. His arms and legs barely moved, roots had sprouted from his pores, his fingernails were curved, and his skin was showing signs of mould. It was only when his cousin said that if he didn't budge he'd call some neighbours to help drag him out of bed that he finally got up. Shrugging off the roots that bound him to the mattress, he moved, after lying in the same place, in the same musty bed, for over a month.

Why do you always focus on the pain? You've always been like this, ever since you were a little girl. Your grandfather's story isn't only one of loss. This story you are telling contains other stories. Why don't you write, for example, about how fortunate he was to set foot in a

country as welcoming as ours? Why don't you say that he was only able to build everything he did because he left? Or that, when he arrived in Brazil, he found a peace that he hadn't previously known? Why insist on words of pain? I can't write any other way. I can be happy too, but not here. Happiness is a part of my life too: in bars, at the beach, with friends, on other journeys. *But why can't you bring it into your writing?* I just can't. If my writing doesn't bleed, it doesn't exist. If it doesn't rend the body, it doesn't exist. I keep returning to pain, because it is what makes me write. *But why don't you try? If you can't write without pain, at least write without this weight, without guilt. Unburden yourself. Be light, let your words be light.* I don't know; I'm not sure I can, but I promise to try.

Do you love me?

Yes.

How much?

You and your questions again!

Answer me: how much?

Very much.

But how very much?

You can't die. It's not fair. I could argue that I'm too young to lose you, that you're too young to leave. That I don't know how to walk without a little of your scent accompanying me, without your tender words to warm me. That I'm still not ready to walk on my own; that I need a little more time. I need a lot of time. All of time. I could argue that there are still too many things we haven't done together. That when I'm sad I won't have your arms to wrap around me. That when I'm afraid I won't have your skirt to hide behind. That I won't have anyone to whom I can say 'I love you' over and over without the slightest fear, without misgivings. I could argue that there are things I've never told you, things I want to tell you. That you too must have stories to tell me. That I want you beside me to hear about the adventures I have yet to live. That I want you by my side when I publish my first book. That I want you by my side when my first child is born, and the second, and the third. I could argue all this and much more, because my desire that you stay is infinite. On the other hand, I know there are arguments for your departure: that's life, it ends, death always comes sooner or later. But I refuse all arguments that are not my own. That's why I cry, wail: Don't go! It's not fair! That's why I shout, as I beat on your coffin of polished wood: Take my mother out of there! I throw my hands in the air like people who aren't right in the head, like the only ones who are right, and repeat: Open the coffin! But everyone is uncomfortable and embarrassed: The poor thing. They pity me, but they don't hear me.

It's a hot, sunny day. When loved ones depart, the days should not be hot and sunny. The gravediggers lower the coffin into the hole and take up large shovels. There are no flowers. There are stones. They cover the coffin with earth, leaving you in there, alone, and me out here, alone. I stop shouting, but I am positive that I am witnessing a great injustice, perhaps the greatest of all. And I think that if you were here everything would be different, that if you were here you'd surely hear me. You'd open the coffin and get out. You'd stand and walk towards me, take my hands, and tell me there's no reason to suffer. If you were here, you'd surely dry the tears rolling from my eyes. But I speak to you and you don't hear me. You can't hear me anymore.

We were in bed when the telephone rang. On the other end, a deep voice asked how I was and said he'd gotten my number from the friend whose party we'd met at the week before. Trying to make conversation, he said: I really enjoyed our talk, however quick, and I would like to get to know you better. I replied in monosyllables, but he was in no hurry to hang up. When he started talking about my eyes and hair, I felt uncomfortable; after all, you were right next to me. I was surprised when, instead of asking me to make up an excuse to end the call, you whispered: don't hang up. You gave me no time to answer or protest. Before I knew it, you had pulled off my clothes, and, as you kneeled in front of me, all I could see was the top of your head. I listened to a stranger's voice as I felt your tongue moistening me. It wasn't easy to control the tone of the conversation, to pay attention to what the guy was saying, or to at least answer: Of course, let's get together sometime. My legs thrashed as I spoke. Worried he'd detect something odd in my voice, I started talking as if I was in a hurry. You noticed and censured me. You wanted to see it through. I had to invent stories, topics, and ask where he'd met our mutual friend and what he did for a living, among other things in which I wasn't even remotely interested. Meanwhile, your tongue became more and more intimate with my vagina, and they slotted together like two mouths kissing. My lower lips felt like my upper ones, incisive, independent, and, most unusually, with a sense of taste. I knew the taste of your tongue so well, but like that, in such an unexpected place, it was completely different. When I eventually hung up, it was because my mouth was between my legs and it would have been strange to go on talking with my lips engaged with yours.

When I was a little girl, my mother told me a story that her father had told her when she was little. From time to time, I find myself leaving the present and returning to this same story, as if it were somehow mine, so great is the terror that it awakens in me. In Istanbul, there was a very large family — generations and generations — that never went anywhere. A family marked by immobility. They suffered when, for some reason, they had to move outside of their habitual territory. They all lived next door to one another, and their houses occupied an entire city block. The Tembers — that was their name — owned grocery stores and tailor shops on the same block. They rarely paid visits, except in exceptional cases. Until one day, in one of the Tember family homes, a fire started. It spread from house to house, until it engulfed the entire block. As usual, they didn't do a thing, and waited for outside help. But the fire was so terrible that no one was prepared to risk their own life to save those of such static individuals. And, thus, the flames devoured the whole family, which, as a result of its paralysis, would never again walk this earth.

His sister's letters became fewer and farther between, which saddened him. Although he was already accustomed to his new life (he had been in Brazil for almost five years now), he still missed his family and some of the things he had left behind. The letters were the only way for him to feel a little closer to it all. Every word brought him a whiff of Turkey, of home. Writing also made him feel closer to his family, and he'd remember Saturdays, when they'd spend hours at the dining table, as if time didn't exist. There was a consensus that on Saturdays no one was allowed to fight, so that, sincere or not, the atmosphere in the house was always one of congeniality and mutual affection. To him, letters were like Saturdays, moments when he felt warm and safe. They didn't always bring good news, it is true, like the one that told of the fate of his beloved Rosa, but for some time now the content of his sister's letters had been more happy than sad: she had fallen in love and become engaged, with their father's blessing; the family was doing well; the older brother had married; everyone was in good health, except for a few aches and pains of their mother's. So, when his sister's letters stopped arriving weekly and became fortnightly, and then monthly, he feared that she was hiding something from him.

He tried not to think about it and went about life as usual, although he kept asking if something was wrong. His sister was always emphatic: *No, dear brother, nothing is wrong. I've just been busy with preparations for the wedding* (she wrote, knowing that she would never marry, her hands shaky with disease, her body lying listlessly on the bed). He wanted to believe her, although he suspected there was a secret lurking among her words, an enormous, dangerous silence. So, when the postman handed him an envelope that didn't have his sister's name on it but his younger brother's, he knew he'd been right: he hadn't been imagining things; the truth was very different to what he'd read in her letters. He tore open the envelope, sensing that the words inside it would be no less painful than those of Rosa's death.

Dear brother,

Unfortunately, I do not have good news. I know that for some time you have been asking if there was something wrong here at home, and if we decided not to tell you anything, it was because our sister wanted it this way. She didn't want to worry you so far from home, and we respected her wishes. I would have preferred to do things differently, because I know that you, like me, prefer the truth, even when it is cruel and sad. But, please understand, it is hard to refuse a request from a loved one when their body is being mercilessly ravaged by disease.

I am writing now because there is no longer anything to hide, no last wish to be fulfilled. We went through seven months of great suffering and, knowing our father as well as you do, you can imagine how we could barely bring up the subject, much less utter the name of the disease. But now I can, I must: it was tuberculosis. She contracted it at the height of her happiness, when she and Samuel had already set their wedding date. You should have seen her, waltzing about the house, laughing at anything, her face rejuvenated, bubbling over with happiness. Until one day she woke up feeling weak, with a strange, scratchy cough. It must be a cold, we thought. Except that instead of getting better, she got worse by the day. When she came back from the doctor's, I realised we'd never see that cheer again. I don't think I've ever seen someone so sad. The atmosphere in the house became so heavy it was as if we'd all begun to stoop, as if we'd all fallen ill with her.

Our house became the saddest in the neighbourhood, filled with the silent suffering of a family that knew it was going to lose its only daughter, and the suffering of that daughter, who believed she'd found happiness. She didn't want to tell you anything, dear brother, because she wanted you to keep believing in a world that no longer existed. Her only moments of happiness were when she received letters from you with news of Brazil, your job, your health, and your friends, and she wanted the feeling to be reciprocal. 'I don't want him to know anything,' she kept telling me, 'because what good would it do? Or do you want him to leave his new home to come visit a sister who isn't long for this world? We can't be selfish,' she insisted. 'Each of us must meet our fate.'

But now, dear brother, I no longer have any reason to hide it from you, as she is no longer among us. I know how much sadness this will bring you, especially because as her twin, you were closest to her. I feel the same pain, and I know how heavy it is. Especially when I think of her sweetness, her grace, and everything she still had in front of her, everything we had yet to do together. Nothing saddens me more than this future that no longer exists.

Our parents are not the same anymore. They stare off into space, as if they've lost their way in the world. I'll never forget Mother standing by the coffin, all in black, with a scarf over her head, like the day you left, but this time singing songs of grief all morning. We all know, even if we haven't been through it ourselves, that there is no pain worse than that of losing a child.

I could carry on for many pages, telling you the details of these long months in which we merely waited for her to die, but I'll spare you this excess, because the truth has been spoken, and it's all that matters. Time will take care of the rest. For now, there is nothing we can do except pray for our dear sister and ask that she be in peace, wherever she is.

Much love,

Sabi

~

When I woke up I was wet, your hand under my skirt, my knickers pulled aside. We were driving around Italy, from north to south. I woke up as if from an erotic dream, but it was your hand, your curious fingers. You were driving fast, with only one hand on the steering wheel, staring at the horizon. I pretended I was still asleep. I curbed my urge to change position, to spread my legs a little or sink further into the seat. I didn't move, but my body was a whirlwind inside. I wonder if you suspected that I was awake. Your finger went faster and faster and I didn't think I'd manage to stay still for long. It was early autumn, the leaves already turning orange. I tried to picture where we were, if we were in the countryside, near the beach, if someone could see us from the highway, if we might get caught in our little misdemeanour. I pictured the situation itself: the two of us in the car, me asleep, you with one hand on the steering wheel, the other touching me. Your finger went faster and faster and I couldn't contain myself.

Shrivelling more and more by the day, my devastated body is no longer mine. It is nothing but viscera, tripe peeking through the cuts where my skin has been gouged away. The stench of sulphur is stronger, and the burden bearing down on my body has become inertia, listlessness. I can smell the worms preparing for the final banquet. I know they are on their way, already anticipating the great feast that will soon begin. Shortly they will be wiggling through me, making new perforations in this body already riddled with holes. With my last iota of energy, I take the typewriter that is pressing down on my belly and place it on the ground. Then I take the two tips of the sheet bunched up at the foot of the bed and pull it over me, covering myself entirely, like a burial shroud.

I couldn't sleep. Whenever I shut my eyes, I knew what it was like not to see, and I didn't want to. I spent nights fighting off sleep, inventing ways to keep my eyes wide open. Even if the room were dark, there would be some faint light coming from outside. Sometimes I'd turn on the lamp and spend the night reading. You didn't even notice. There were so many injections, you were on so much medication that, come night, you'd crash. Meanwhile, I did what I could to stay awake, because I was afraid to wake up and discover that something had changed. When you woke up, my heart would start to race. Can you see what time it is? We always did the same test. In front of you was a wall clock with large numbers. If you were able to tell me what time it was, everything was okay. Then all we had to do was wait for another day to pass. *I knew the battle was coming to an end and it was time*

to lay down my weapons. Your fear peaks when you're in the midst of the fight, but when you know there is nothing more you can do, it fades. I wasn't afraid anymore. I was beside myself, I'd never felt so panicked. It was worse than if I had lost my own sight: it was you who was losing it, and there I was, unable to do a thing. I wanted to understand exactly what you were feeling, to be in your place. *In my place? And what would you have done?* I don't know, but I wanted to know what your pain was like and I couldn't. My heart was filled with anxiety. Whenever I closed my eyes, I felt a little of your suffering. It seemed so enormous that I'd open them quickly. It wasn't fair that you should have to go through that. *I won't say I didn't suffer. That would be a lie. But I also felt the deepest joy in that hospital. The two of us in that same room for two weeks. I had never felt love so explicitly before. Every gesture, no matter how small, had the intensity of a declaration. Devoid of fear and angst, I could feel everything you had to offer me. Love. Is there any greater joy? You lying next to me in the hospital bed, against the rules. You reading me that epistolary novel, remember? The two of us playing cards, when I was still able to. You letting me win, as parents do with small children. You keeping tabs on my drip. You telling me about your adventures. You making sure the nurses followed the doctor's orders to a T. You giving me sponge baths, applying ointment to my vagina, touching my body covered with sores, riddled with holes, filled with pus, with its acidic smell, its smell of death. You touching me without disgust, as if my body were yours, ours.* It's true, you're right. I didn't know the extent of our love either. It was as if we stretched it a little each day and the further we did, the more we understood that it would go as far as we wanted it to. It had no boundaries, no limits. It was a presence that was stronger than the vulnerability of the flesh. It was timeless, and only later, after I'd stopped fearing your death, did I understand that, back then, it was still mixed with pain. Now I know the precise meaning of that love. Now, Mother, it is me who carries you in my belly.

I was leaving the bathroom when you forced me back in. Facing the mirror, I admired the reflection of your face as you nudged my legs apart.

I was ambling along in Istanbul's scalding heat when I came across a cucumber stall. An elderly man was skilfully peeling them and selling each one for a few cents. Small, medium, and large cucumbers. Whole, with nothing but salt. I was amazed — it was the first time I'd seen anything like it. At the same time, nothing could have been more familiar: salted cucumbers, to be eaten as rabbits eat carrots in cartoons. When I was a girl, I refused to eat lunch or dinner without first having a cucumber, whole, with salt. For an afternoon snack, a cucumber. I'd like one, please, I told the man.

How big?

Small, I said. They're the best, crunchier.

I asked if I could have my picture taken with him, behind the stall. It was funny: the man was serious, focused, his long moustache following the closed contour of his mouth, while I wore a goofy grin, pleased with my discovery. I began to think that, yes, the trip was for a reason. The past wasn't my grandfather's alone, it didn't belong only to those who had emigrated. The cucumber was proof.

After his sister's death, his younger brother wrote him a few more letters, all tinged with the dried blood of the departed. He no longer looked forward to the postman's visit. That is, until the day his brother wrote, not to talk about the household in mourning, but a decision he'd made: *I'm coming to Brazil, to join you. My time has come.* Happiness inflated his chest, made him feel light and fresh, like a rain shower on a hot summer's day. He would receive Sabi in the land that was now his, and he'd help him to get established, to grow as he had grown. Yes, he could help his brother make something of his life, and the thought filled him with enthusiasm. Good news at last!

On the day of his brother's arrival, he didn't go to work, asking an employee to cover for him (by this time he already had his own hardware shop). He rose early, showered, dabbed on his best fragrance — as if he were going to court a woman — and put on a suit and tie, because he wanted to greet his brother in style. He was so nervous that his stomach churned and he could barely eat breakfast. He hurried out, wanting to arrive at Praça Mauá before ten o'clock, when the ship was due to dock. He spent almost two hours in the blazing sun, staring anxiously at the horizon, trying to catch sight of a large ship like the one that had brought him to Brazil years earlier.

He was almost nodding off on a bench in the square when he heard the whistle he was waiting for: it was him, his brother, arriving. He raced to the edge of the pier to wave so his brother would know he was there. While the hull of the ship made waves in the water, he waved and shouted: Sabi, Sabi! His brother waved back with his felt hat. How different he was, all grown up. A man already!

After a long embrace, they kissed each other on the cheeks, both dripping with sweat. They laughed, cried. *Mazel tov*, they repeated, wishing each other good luck, luck in their new land.

Sabi seemed mature, and was willing to do whatever was necessary so as not to regret his choice. My grandfather was proud of him; his feelings toward his younger brother were fatherly. He knew he'd have to help and look out for Sabi a lot, but he didn't mind. On the contrary, it gave him a renewed vigour, a happiness he'd felt few times in his life.

He helped Sabi carry his suitcases and accompanied him to immigration, where Sabi filled in forms and presented his documentation. He had taken out Brazilian citizenship, which made it easier for Sabi to get a visa. It took a while, nevertheless. The queue was long, and the questions, interminable. But when they finally exited, Sabi holding his papers, they left the bother of the wait and the heat behind. They had too much to tell each other to worry about bureaucratic trifles. He wanted to know how their father, mother, and brother were, how the voyage had been, if Sabi was okay, and if he was willing to start work the next day. Sabi wanted to know how things worked in Rio de Janeiro, where he was going to live, if it was hard to learn Portuguese, and if he could start work the next day.

But there was no hurry; there was plenty of time. They had their future in front of them, together — a future graced with good fortune, unexpected events, love, families, and work, lots of hard work. Like all futures, it would also bring pain and loss, but what did it matter at that moment? All they wanted to do was catch up, be brothers again, make up for all the time in which they'd missed each other. And plan the future, even if later it turned out to be different than they'd imagined.

I don't know if there was a specific moment when the fights started. Perhaps they were always inherent to us. Just as we couldn't live without each other physically, we also couldn't live without fighting. Sometimes we hurt each other. We almost always broke up. You almost always did the breaking up, because I wouldn't have known what to do with my body without yours. In all truth, you wouldn't have either, but it was a part of your act to show me that, unlike me, you could live well on your own — you would live better on your own. Every time you thought I was getting too clingy, you'd say: this isn't working, I don't want this, you ask too much of me, I need some time, we both need to live our own lives. I'd get desperate, and shout: my life is yours, my life is ours. And for hours we'd play out what to an onlooker was just an act, but to me was death itself. Until eventually the spiteful words gave way to sweet words. And the sweet words transmuted into sweet (desperate) kisses, sweet (desperate) touches, and sweet (desperate) caresses. Then we'd make (sweet, desperate) love, like never before. We'd devour each other as if we'd just met, as if we held no grudges. Our sweaty bodies on the bed, the room smelling of sex. After a long time we'd have a cold shower, and it would be as if we were two children, as if we'd never fought, as if we'd never broken up, as if we'd always belonged to each other, as if we always would belong to each other.

At the entrance, none of the women spoke English. It was evident from their sideways glances that my presence was unusual: they didn't get many foreigners there. Nevertheless, it didn't take too much gesticulating to make them understand that I wanted to come in. It had taken me a while to find a traditional Turkish bath, frequented only by Muslim women. On the bus, I had approached a woman and timidly asked if she could recommend a nearby *hammam*. They're for tourists. Turkish women haven't gone to *hammams* for a long time, she laughed. Embarrassed, I went to find a place at the back of the bus. But before getting off, almost as if regretting her indelicacy, she handed me a piece of paper with a name on it: *Yildiz*. You'll find what you're looking for there, she said.

The woman at reception pointed at my clothes, indicating that I should take them off. I did as two girls beside me did, removing my garments one by one, leaving on only my underwear, and placing them on a shelf in the corridor that led to the baths. A woman who spoke a few words of English came over to ask if I wanted one of the services she was offering: a massage or exfoliation. It is part of the Islamic cleansing ritual to scrub the skin to remove what is dead. I accepted both. She took me by the hand and led me through the curtain into the baths. I got a shock: it was nothing like what I'd imagined. Of course I hadn't expected to find myself in a five-star hotel — after all, I'd chosen to go to a traditional bath — but I had no idea it would be such a mess and, above all, so dirty. Scattered about the floor were hairs, empty shampoo bottles, and soap wrappers, and the room was awash with dark water. The heat was infernal. I hesitated for a second and almost did an about-turn: I'm so sorry, but I have to go, I forgot I have to be somewhere. But I controlled the impulse and told myself: if these women are here, looking so alive and happy, why can't I be? If I really wanted to experience their world, I'd have to leave mine at the door.

What's your name? I asked.

Sihem.

What?

Sihem.

It took me some effort and three or four tries to pronounce her name correctly. She knew I was nervous. It was obvious: my eyes were shot with fear. I felt like bursting into tears at that moment, begging someone to get me out of there. She too felt uneasy, though less than I did, which was why she was almost able to disguise it. We came from two different worlds, and our awkwardness with each other was a constant reminder that I was a foreigner. But we slowly bridged the gap, and I began to feel more at ease, willing to participate in the stages of the ritual.

There must have been ten or twelve women there. They all, without exception, stared at me unabashedly. They laughed among themselves, whispering words that I didn't understand. I couldn't tell if they were happy about my presence or not. Although I didn't want to be, the truth is that I was an intruder. Sihem was still holding my hand. We crossed the first room, which wasn't as hot, and went to the second, where the exfoliation would take place. She gave me a plastic mat to sit on so I wouldn't come into contact with the ground. I sat on it (not without a little revulsion) and hugged my legs to my chest. While I waited, Sihem filled a bucket of water, mixing hot and cold. Suddenly, she threw the water over me all at once. I hadn't expected it. The water went into my nostrils and I began to cough. She was unfazed and went about her work without hesitation. Using soap paste, she scrubbed my body from head to toe. I relaxed a little and even thought that the soap, which made my skin slippery, felt nice. Then I had another bucket of water thrown over me, but this time I held my breath.

The others were doing to one another what Sihem was doing to me: they all scrubbed, exfoliated, and threw water over one another. Only one older woman was bathing alone, over by the wall to the left of the room. She was chubby, her belly spilling over in rolls. I wondered if that was why no one was helping her. Maybe. But maybe not. Maybe she was unhappy. Or maybe she just liked being alone. I imagined a story for each of the women around me. I invented husbands, betrayals, children, travels, work, loneliness; I invented sadness and happiness; I envied them and felt relieved I wasn't one of them.

One of the women caught my eye. Long, brown hair, fleshy lips. She was younger than most of the others there, soaping herself as if she were caressing her body. She didn't say a word, but interacted with whomever she had to. Her body was perfect, with the most beautiful breasts I had ever seen, ever wanted to touch. Small, round nipples. A sensual body that didn't care if it was sensual. I tried not to be conspicuous, but she noticed. I was afraid to invade her space, to be inconvenient. She made it clear that no, I wasn't being inconvenient. On the contrary, she stared at me too, studied me with the same lack of shame. Amid bodies oblivious to sexuality, bodies merely given over to cleansing, we established our bond.

Sihem shook my feet. She wanted me to lie on my back, which I did without hesitation. She started scrubbing me with a glove, so hard that I thought my skin would bleed. With worried eyes, waving my hand, I asked her to be gentler. She laughed and, ignoring my request, went back to work, as if to say that I didn't understand a thing. If the choice to be there was mine, I'd have to surrender to the experience and leave my own customs outside. She didn't say a word, but she didn't need to either. She merely led me through the process as she saw fit, unconcerned that my wishes might be different. I resolved to put an end to the stand-off. Trying to impose my own ideas on her would get me nowhere. I decided to relax and make the most of it. Not least because I soon got used to the scrubbing and it stopped hurting. It even felt nice on my legs and tickled a little.

When she finished exfoliating me, Sihem made me stand and look at the ground. Pieces of skin were scattered about like lengths of string. See all that spaghetti? I laughed. Spaghetti? It did bear some resemblance, but it was weird imagining pieces of spaghetti being sloughed off my body. She made a point of showing me that I had much more dead skin than the other women, as if to say: See how clean we are? It struck me as slightly ironic. After all, when I arrived the place had seemed so terribly filthy, and suddenly there I was being accused of uncleanliness. I was dirty because I had more pieces of 'spaghetti' than the others.

Still mesmerised by the beauty of the young woman I had just discovered, I imagined what it would be like to touch her radiant skin, because after exfoliation it is smoother, softer. Our connection was explicit. She smiled at my awkwardness, at how ill at ease I was with such a new experience, and I smiled in response, happy that she was there, in the same room, witness to my first Turkish bath. I smiled at her beauty, enchanted by her delicacy, almost laughing out loud: I had never seen such a beautiful woman before.

As I stood up, another bucket of water was thrown over me. I already felt confident enough to scrub my own body in front of everyone. I asked Sihem if I could pour the bucket over myself. She filled it again and handed it to me with a self-satisfied look, certain that the fact I was enjoying the ritual was her achievement. I noticed the other women looking at me, and some of them started to give me some tips, explaining what I should do through gestures. I imitated them diligently. Suddenly, one walked over, handed me her glove and asked me to scrub her back. I trembled. I didn't have the slightest idea how to do it. I was afraid. She sat there waiting for me to exfoliate her, as Sihem had just done to me. Tired of waiting, she turned around, took back her glove, and waved her hands in the air, explaining what I was supposed to do. Nothing complicated; all I had to do was start. The glove was rough and a certain amount of pressure had to be applied for it to be effective. I felt as if I was hurting her, but it was evident that

I wasn't. She was used to it and probably came to the *hammam* once a week, as was the custom in her religion. I was already growing tired when she asked for the glove back and gave me a smile of approval.

In the other room, the heat was more bearable. That was where I was given the massage. Lying on my belly, I felt Sihem's hands working the knots out of my muscles. I was tense, as usual. My lower back hurt, my neck and shoulders were stiff, rocks embedded in my body. Are you carrying the world on your shoulders? she asked me. I told her that people always asked me that, but no, it wasn't the world. I was carrying my past, I was carrying a story that wasn't mine, which was why I was there in Turkey. I told her that my grandfather had emigrated from Smyrna. That I was there in search of my past and to look for the old family home. She listened with attention and it was as if in that moment we became equals for the first time.

So you're Turkish?

Not exactly.

Do you speak Turkish?

No.

Not at all?

Absolutely nothing.

But you're Turkish anyway. You look Turkish — I had already noticed your features.

Crack, crack, went my bones and I sighed with relief. She was a little heavy-handed for my small body, and I was a bit uncomfortable, but there was no way I was going to complain, much less now that our connection had been legitimised. After I told her why I was in Turkey, she made the massage even more intense, as if doing her part to help me free myself of the past. I felt that she wasn't just loosening up my muscles, but also fighting against everything I had just told her.

The young woman left while I was lying on my belly. I didn't even have a chance to say goodbye, to look into her eyes one last time. By the time Sihem finished the massage, the woman had simply gone. Anxiously, I looked for her. She couldn't have disappeared like that. How could I continue my journey without her? Without those breasts that I had never touched? Without the mouth that I had never kissed? No, she couldn't have left without saying goodbye to me.

I think Sihem had spent more time with me than was usual. I was exhausted from the trip, from so many new things. Exhausted just to think about what lay ahead of me. Would I find my ancestors' home? Would the key still be the same? I tried to believe in the story I had invented for myself, a story that I was still inventing — the only one capable of providing me with any answers, perhaps the craziest story of all, but also the most real. I didn't know to what extent my grandfather's stories were true, to what extent what I was experiencing now was true. I didn't even know if my journey was real. It seemed that the closer I got to the facts, the further I got from the truth.

Today I masturbated thinking about you with another woman. For heaven's sake, am I going mad?

We weren't in the hospital anymore, but in a hotel in the city of Baltimore, in the United States. I thought you were still asleep and opened the curtain only a crack, so as not to wake you. Outside, the city glimmered. You heard me moving about the room and asked if I was up. Yes, it's almost nine o'clock, I said, glancing at the clock on the nightstand. Your eyes were closed. I'm going to open the curtains, I said. It's a beautiful day out. You didn't say a thing, and it occurred to me that I was the one who shouldn't have said anything. I saw you opening your eyes and then closing them, opening them again, closing them again. That was when it dawned on me that maybe it made no difference, and I realised that your open eyes didn't linger on anything. They were like two lost marbles, like an instrument that you didn't know how to use. I saw it, and I didn't say anything. I watched you and noticed that as I looked at you, you didn't look at me. We'd never look into each other's eyes again. Like in a film in fast motion, I began to imagine everything that you'd never see again: the sun outside; the cities of the world, with people walking, bumping into one another, hurrying past, or just strolling along; the dogs; the birds. You'd never again see Rio de Janeiro, Ipanema, Copacabana, the beach, the sunset, the moon rising over the ocean, the trees. You'd never again watch films; you'd never read another book. And when my hair grew long or when I cut it off, or when I bought new clothes, or put on weight, or got pregnant, or grew old, you wouldn't see it. You wouldn't see a thing. Ever again.

Mother? I blurted out, almost shouting, as if calling for help. Mother? I said, almost crying, almost collapsing, as if hearing you speak might stop me.

Yes? you said, without any enthusiasm in your voice.

I think I'm going to get something to eat, a sandwich or some yoghurt. What would you like?

Anything, you said. I'm not hungry.

Okay, maybe I'll buy some fruit, a banana or an apple, I said as I got dressed, my eyes full of tears. I just wanted to get out of the room so I could cry without you hearing me. And I did, from the hotel corridor until the moment I returned with two sandwiches and a banana. When I came back, you were still lying in bed, in the same position, opening and closing your eyes. I left the paper bag on the table next to the television and lay down next to you. We didn't touch the food.

Mother? I said, this time in a steady voice, as if my tears had carried away my fear.

What? you said, eyes wide open, unblinking.

You can't see anything anymore, can you?

You didn't answer, just shut your eyes, and it was your mouth that cried, your downturned lips. Then I hugged you tightly, very tightly, and said: Everything will be okay, you'll see. I listed all the things you could do without seeing: there was still lots of music to listen to; I'd read you stories, newspapers, novels, poetry; we could talk a lot, eat yummy things, and drink good wines; you could dictate to me everything that you wanted to write; you could imagine all the films that you wouldn't see, because in your head you could still see lots and lots, you could still see whatever you wanted. Lying there like that, you listening in silence as I enumerated all the things you could do, we invented a world for ourselves for the last time, we created the world we would live in for the last time. We still didn't know that in two weeks it would all be gone, that in two weeks you wouldn't be able to see or imagine, or listen to music, or taste good wines, or hug me, or hear the many many stories that I wanted to tell you.

I had two names on a piece of paper: Raphael and Salomon. The surname was exactly the same as mine. These were the people I had to look up when I got to Smyrna. According to my grandfather, it wouldn't be hard to find them, because it was a small community and he'd received news of them only a few years earlier from some cousins in France. Yes, maybe the channels would be open and I'd find them easily, but then what? What was I supposed to do after I located them? I was afraid I wouldn't know what to say, that I wouldn't have anything to talk about with those people of whom I knew nothing. I knew that in some way, at some point, we crossed paths on the same family tree. But what did they do? What did they think? How did they live? Would we have any affinities, subjects of mutual interest? Or would they be as foreign to me as the people I saw in the streets of Istanbul, as the people I had come across by chance and whom I would probably never see again? I was hesitant, but at the same time anxious to find out what was going to happen on this journey, in the story I was telling myself.

When you leaned over to whisper sweetly in my ear, I knew you were going to ask me to do something: Tomorrow, I want you to go out for the day and only come back in the evening. I want you to wear a miniskirt without anything underneath. Yes, you heard me: I want you completely naked underneath.

This journey is a lie: I've never left this musty bed. My body rots a little more each day, I'm riddled with pustules, and soon I'll be nothing but bones. My legs are covered in weeping wounds and my flesh is raw. How could I undertake such a journey? I have no joints; my bones are fused to one another. The only way I could leave this bed is if someone were to carry me, but who would pick up such a repugnant body? What for? I have the silence and solitude of an entire family in me, of generations and generations. As if all the happy things that they all lived had dissipated into the air, leaving only the sad ones. When I was born, my parents took one look at me and knew that I was sadness and solitude. That after me there would be nothing, because after sadness and solitude there is nothing. Ever since I was a girl, it's always been the same: whenever someone looks at me, I see fear cross their face, because I came into the world old and I carry death in my eyes.

I have never left the spot, I have never travelled, I know nothing but the darkness of my room. The key my grandfather gave me is still beside me, lying on the bed as if it were part of my putrid body. We are both the colour of worn bronze, covered in dust. It is as if we were one, so rusted that, in a person's hand, we would be nothing but dust, lumps of flesh, and shards of metal.

Don't you ever think about positive things? Don't you have any dreams? I do, of course I do. I dream that one day a prince will come to fetch me on a white horse. I won't need to make any effort. He'll know that I'm the woman he has been looking for. All we'll have to do is look at each other to know we were made for one another. He'll offer me his hand and take me, on horseback, to a beautiful place, where there will be a big party, where I will be reunited with everyone who has already departed this world and everyone that is still in it. We'll live happily there, in a land that knows no death, no time, no pain. *So you dream?* Of course I dream. I have another dream that I've never told anyone. *What is it?* My dream, Mother, is to write. *To write?* Yes, I have this impossible dream: to write and write and write.

He had sworn never to love another woman and, although he wished he could undo his promise, it was what ended up happening. When he saw Hilda at the club dance, he knew he would make a home with her. He also knew that he would cultivate affection and admiration for her, but never the love he had felt for Rosa. He had two left feet, and stepped on Hilda's toes. He didn't know the music had a beat to follow. The invitation (Let's sit down a little?) was a way to avoid another such disaster. Hilda wasn't especially beautiful (short, slightly hunched shoulders, long nose, crooked fingers), but she was attractive in her own way, with the charm of a woman who was quick to smile, at peace with life. And that was what drew him to her; he wanted someone cheerful by his side. He asked her how old she was, if she came to the club often, and if he could see her the following week.

The second time they saw each other, they didn't dance to a single song. They just talked. He asked about her family, where she was from, her father's profession, and where they lived. The third time, again at the club, he asked if she was single. The fourth, in Lido Square, if she would like to marry him. The fifth, in Machado Square, if he could talk to his future father-in-law to ask for her hand in marriage. The sixth, at their home, Hilda hung back, watching her almost-fiancé talk to her father. The seventh, the eighth, the ninth, the tenth, and the eleventh, they talked about the wedding and the future. The twelfth time they saw each other, she drank from the wine the rabbi handed her, and he broke the glass, the noise of the splinters on the ground confirming that they would be connected for life, until death did they part.

He and Hilda were a couple like many others. His business began to grow, with increasingly satisfactory profits, and he decided to expand the shop. He remained in the same downtown shopping district he'd been in from the start, but moved to a bigger establishment. At home, Hilda fell pregnant for the first time: they hoped for a boy to carry on the family business. He hired new employees to help in the shop, which was even busier. She suffered from morning sickness, and missed having company in the house. He worked late into the night at the shop. His ambitions were great. She felt her belly growing at a frightening pace. He barely saw her, and would arrive home with bookkeeping to do, his mind elsewhere. Her eyes teared up when she felt her baby's feet kick for the first time. He was euphoric about the shop's profits. She gave birth on a hot March day. He was there, heart beating wildly, when the doctor came out of the delivery room to give him the good news: it was a boy. His kingdom was guaranteed.

By the time their second child (a girl) came along, the shop already had a branch in Copacabana, and the family had moved to a house in the now-affluent neighbourhood of Leblon —

which, at the time, was madness: Leblon? But it's so far away, so deserted … The girl came at a good time, because Hilda was aching for a companion. The daughter would keep her company as she starched collars, cooked dinner, and dusted the house. The son, in turn, was already a little king, demanding his mother's constant attention and pampering.

They were well-off by the time Hilda fell pregnant for the third time: another girl. He was a little disappointed at the news, while she was happy with what fate had given her, a new ally around the house. By now, the shop had another three branches in different parts of town, and no longer sold only tools, but all kinds of construction materials. This success in business ensured the family many privileges, such as an imported car, a driver, and two maids; and for the children, a bilingual school, and private piano and French lessons. The third child was born into the bosom of a family that was so successful it barely remembered the past. The suffering and hardship the father had endured before he was married were not to be mentioned. After all, what mattered now was that they were well, with good health, work, and harmony. Everything else was the past, and the past had to be silenced, left dormant among the threads of memory.

No one was surprised when Hilda fell pregnant for the fourth time. An affluent family should proliferate. The second boy came into the world on the last day of an atypically harsh winter in

Rio de Janeiro. But he was terribly weak, with underdeveloped lungs, and lived only three days. He never saw the family home and barely spent any time in his mother's arms. My grandfather raged in the corridors, talked to himself, saying *mazel bajo* — it can only be God's punishment. He felt deeply guilty, although he was guilty of nothing. It must have been a divine curse for some sin of his own. But why the boy? he repeated, unafraid and unashamed that his daughters might hear him.

Four years passed, and silence and mourning reigned in the house. The boy's ghost lurked in every room and, like the past, no one was allowed to talk about him. If someone mentioned him, even if only briefly, it would bring on a fit of paternal fury. As if it was disrespectful of his pain. Until, on another winter's day, Hilda revealed that she was pregnant again. They would have another boy, it was certain.

Wary of a second divine punishment, he curbed his urge to shout at the heavens when he walked into the hospital room and saw another girl in his wife's arms. After a dead boy, a girl. There she was, fragile, trying to suck a little of her mother's milk, and she could never have imagined how strong she would have to be in life. It was as if her body contained a secret that would only be revealed years later. Even as an adult, when she had to face the dictatorship and, later, cancer, she never lost the fragility that was evident in her tiny baby's body.

Her father thought he didn't love her, because she reminded him of his dead son. Only when she was taken prisoner by the dictatorship and he feared he might lose her did he finally understand that his love was old, and that the ties that united them had been established at the hospital, the same day he had almost cursed fate for having brought him another girl.

When you leaned over to whisper sweetly in my ear, I knew you were going to ask me to do something: Think of a woman. I closed my eyes and sought in my memory for a female body that excited me. Have you thought of someone?

Wait, I said, and was immediately surprised by your face between my legs. With my eyes closed, I thought of the most beautiful breasts I had ever seen, ever wanted to touch. Small, round nipples. Maybe you, certain I was thinking about a woman, were thinking about her too. The same one or another one. And we made love untiringly, all over the flat. Then we lay on the bed and you asked who I had thought about, if she was real, what she looked like. Blonde? Brunette? If I'd ever made love with a woman, if I was attracted to women. Then we started all over again, you, excited by my answers, and I, excited to be telling you my stories, to invent stories.

It was the first time I had prayed. I didn't know what to do, how to do it, but I prayed. I asked God, if he existed, not to let the phone ring. I prayed quietly, whispering, with my hands clasped together in front of my chest. I prayed for the phone never to ring so I wouldn't have to pick up, hear the person on the other end telling me what had happened. I prayed: don't ring don't ring don't ring. I prayed: please God, if you exist, don't take her away from me. Please don't let the phone ring, never ever. But it did: one, two, three, four, five, six, seven, eight, nine, ten, eleven, twelve times, I counted, telling myself: it's not ringing, I can't hear it, it's not ringing. Then it stopped, and for a few seconds I believed it hadn't rung. Until I heard a voice inside the flat, a roar, a cry of despair, and thought: He doesn't exist, God doesn't exist. It had been the phone, it had rung, there was no avoiding it. I hadn't been the one to pick up, I hadn't heard the voice on the other end, but it had all happened. My body buckled, my torso bent over my legs, I felt like I was going to faint, and then, as if hanging on to the last stretch of rope, I roared too, echoing the voice in the other room. I let out a wail, a howl that faltered, a voice in ruins.

There was nothing more I could do, not even pray.

I was heading for the city centre when the long black hair of a woman on the other side of the street caught my eye. Was it her? I couldn't get her beauty out of my mind. I thought about her obsessively. Yes, it's her, I thought, the woman from the *hammam*. Hypnotised, I crossed the street without looking either way, hurrying so I wouldn't lose sight of her. In the morning there were so many people in the street that it wouldn't have been hard. I bumped into people and stumbled, anxious to keep up. When she left the crowd and turned onto a wide footpath, I thought, with relief, that she wasn't going to escape me. She was wearing a long skirt and a tank top. Under her arm, she was carrying a folder that was neither large nor small. She wasn't far from me now.

As I stepped through a door in a large wall, I realised we had just entered the Grand Bazaar, a kind of walled-off district, with its own streets and corners. But it was an area where there were only shops, rows and rows of them. It wasn't long before the shopkeepers started inviting me into their businesses. Some asked: Spanish? Italian? Portuguese? The funnier ones said: Chinese? Japanese?

She walked along quickly, oblivious to her surroundings. I quickened my pace and positioned myself diagonally in front of her. When I looked back, certain of finding the same gaze as the other day, I was unable to hide my disappointment. She stared me firmly in the eye, as if to say: What are you looking at? Unintimidated, I merely responded with a look of frustration.

After she walked away, I lost myself in the bazaar, like a stray dog. I heard the voices of the shopkeepers coming from all sides. They all stood outside their shops, trying to catch the attention of passers-by. When someone showed an interest, they went inside to show them their wares, ever ready to reveal the secrets and qualities of each item.

I was drawn to one shop by the colours, the lighting. It sold only candleholders, of every shape and size. Some to sit on tables, others to hang, others to rest on the ground like glass mosaics of alternating colours: red, blue, green, orange, yellow. They were small glass hexagons held together by a kind of plaster. Contrary to other shops of the sort, this one had lit candles in almost every holder, to attract prospective buyers. I stood at the entrance admiring them all, and a man came out to greet me. He told me that there were different kinds inside and invited me in. The shop was small but adorable. The objects were arranged well and I was truly enchanted by what I saw. The man observed me without speaking. It was hard to pick one. They were all beautiful and at the same time similar. I chose one almost randomly and asked how much it was. It was one to hang from the ceiling, and looked old-fashioned, reminding me of the palaces I had visited. Thirty euros, he told me.

I smiled and said: I don't have euros, I'm Brazilian. I had already been warned not to buy anything without bargaining, as they never give you the real price.

Thirty-five Turkish liras, he said.

It's too much, I insisted.

Thirty, he said.

Twenty, I said.

Twenty-five, I can't do it for any less.

Okay, I said, twenty-five.

I left the shop with the wrapped candleholder in a plastic bag and continued strolling casually through the bazaar. The most beautiful shops were those selling spices, with enormous bags displaying chillies, saffron, paprika, herbs, dried fruits, olives, pistachios, and a vast array of Turkish sweets. Like so many other customers, I tasted a little of each, and ended up buying a bag of rose-flavoured Turkish delights to eat as I wandered.

I kept walking, also fascinated by the shops selling silver and gold. Some looked very expensive. Others seemed to sell only costume jewellery, although they assured me that all their pieces were genuine. Many items were in several of the shops, with the same design — the same red, blue, or green stones, and strands of ornate silver dangling from earrings and necklaces. There was a ring called a harem ring: it had four narrow loops of silver or gold set with colourful little stones that, all together, formed a relatively large piece. I asked why it was called that and was told that it brought luck in love and helped you find a husband. I smiled. I passed many shops. It was hard to exit them, because the shop assistants insisted, argued, haggled, and weren't content if I didn't buy anything.

But suddenly, in one such shop, a long, oval-shaped ring caught my eye. It was made with dark silver to look old, with a green stone in the centre. I asked if the silver and the stone were genuine, and the shopkeeper assured me that they were. I only had his word to go on and decided to trust him. The ring was a little big, but the man said he could adjust it. I asked when it would be ready, and he said the same day, later that afternoon. When he was measuring my finger, he noticed the ring on my other hand. It's beautiful, he said. Where did you buy it?

It was my mother's, I said. And if I'm not mistaken, she bought it in Egypt. See all these little holes? There used to be a green stone in each one.

If you want, I can set it with new stones, he offered.

I hesitated, afraid it might not look nice. I'm not sure, I said. It was like this when I got it. And to be honest, I like things that have gone, that aren't here anymore. I like ruins, secrets of the past. I don't like restored things, as if they were built yesterday. I prefer marks, vestiges. Then I added: My mother bought this ring over thirty years ago. Do you think mine will last that long too? One day I'd like to give it to a daughter of my own.

Yes, he said, and guaranteed that it would last a long time. I'm just not sure about the stone, he joked. That I can't promise. And we both laughed.

When you leaned over to whisper sweetly in my ear, I knew you were going to ask me to do something and I pulled away, tired of your requests. You pretended not to notice and leaned towards me again. I said: No, I don't want to hear it, I'm tired of your requests. You held me tightly by the wrists, with just one hand. I shouted: Let go of me! You didn't. You picked up a pencil that was lying nearby and ran its sharp tip down my arm. Blood trickled out onto the sofa. Like a madwoman, I hollered that you were a psychopath, mentally ill, that you hit women, that I was going to the police, that I hated you, you disgusted me, turned my stomach. When you let go, I pushed you with all the strength I could muster and, with my index finger hovering in front of your face, said without blinking: Next time I'll pluck your eyes out. Both of them.

The pale blue face of the deceased, nostrils stopped up with cotton, and the last smile of death are things I can only imagine. I've never seen a dead body, nor did I see you dead. I saw you dying, asking for water to wet your dry throat, saying you were thirsty, and the nurse telling me that I couldn't give you any. I was torn, afraid to give you water and do you harm, afraid you'd die of thirst if I didn't — lost in my fear, a little girl about to lose her mother, not knowing what to do (if there were only one kind of pain in the world, it would be that of seeing someone you love perish and not being able to do a thing). You were still here, air still entering and leaving your lungs, but I knew that shortly we wouldn't be together anymore; shortly the warm hand I was holding would grow cold and indifferent to my warmth. The doctor had already warned me: It's only a matter of time. He didn't say: Your mother is dead. He said: Your mother is going to die. She is alive, breathing, her heart is beating, her blood is circulating, her eyes open and close, but soon it will all be just a memory, soon her organs will stop working and she will die. It's only a matter of time. I felt like replying: But she's here, she's breathing, she's alive, so there's still time, not to wait for her to die, but to do something to avoid it. You see, it's almost logical: if she's still here, then she can stay. But I knew there was no logic in this reasoning; in fact, it wasn't even reasoning — it was my foolish desire, my colossal fear of losing you.

I went home with the bags under my eyes almost trailing on the ground, my hunched shoulders transforming me into a hook. It's only a matter of time, the doctor's voice echoed in my thoughts. I didn't see you die; I didn't see you dead. It was the telephone ringing that told me we'd never look into each other's eyes again, we'd never embrace or exchange loving words again. The telephone and the cry of pain coming from somewhere in the flat. We were only in the same room again the next day at the cemetery, you inside the coffin of polished wood, with the lid closed — because we bury our dead without clothes on, so they may return to the earth as they came into the world, so the end may be the same as the beginning. I wanted to open the coffin and yell: *Take my mother out of there!* But they didn't listen. They didn't want to listen. And that is why I didn't see you dead. All I saw was the coffin that was to carry you under the earth and which, from that moment on, would be your new home.

After a long night of insomnia, I came to the conclusion that I had nothing left to do in Istanbul. The city was beautiful and I could have stayed on for many days, but the longer I stayed, the more I distanced myself from the objective of my journey.

I headed downstairs to reception and asked for help to contact an airline. I'd like to go to Smyrna today, I said.

There wasn't much time before I had to leave for the airport. I decided to go out for a wander near the hotel, have an orange juice, and say goodbye to the city that was already a little mine. The sun was hotter than it had been on the previous days, and everything looked even more turquoise than it actually was. I liked to look at people's faces, their expressions of tiredness, enthusiasm, happiness, sadness, and boredom. But despite the variety of facial features and cultural differences, I felt as if they were all one, and that it didn't matter if I was in Istanbul or Rio. I may have been wrong (many people would tell me so), but that is what I thought as I drank my juice at an outdoor table, on a narrow street around the corner from the hotel.

Unhurriedly, I paid the young man who had served me and returned to my room. I wanted to call my grandfather before I left. We had spoken when I arrived, but not since. I imagined that he was anxious for news. He, more than anyone, was praying for everything to go smoothly; after all, it was he who was accompanying me — his story, his memory.

On the other end of the line, I heard his cheerful voice: How's my sugar plum?

Well, thanks. I have so much to tell you. I'm dazzled by Istanbul.

So tell me. Where have you been? What have you been up to?

So many things…

I told him everything, every detail of the things I had seen, the smells and flavours I had discovered, the colours of the city, the people. As he listened he expressed his delight, as if he were in my place. We were about to hang up when he asked: What about Smyrna, when are you going?

Actually, that's why I called, to say I'm going today.

His silence struck me as odd. No sign of enthusiasm?

But then I heard his voice, a little choked up, but strong. It sounded very far away: That's good, darling, that's good.

We hung up, and I called the receptionist to ask him to arrange a taxi. I was anxious to go. Smyrna awaited me.

When the rabbi came over with the scissors, I pointed to my heart and said: Here. I was supposed to wear the black blouse with a cut on the left side for seven days, in memory of the dead. And then throw it into the sea. It is still draped across my body, out of fear or fatigue — I'm not sure which.

When she arrived he was lost in thought, sprawled across the bed, while a solitary cigarette burned in the ashtray. He sat up suddenly: So, how was it? He had stayed at home (he couldn't risk being seen) while she had gone to the meeting. It was all much of a muchness, she replied in the same monotone as always. He sighed in relief (he had feared bad news) and said: Let's eat. They went to the kitchen to rummage through the cupboard for some pasta and tomato sauce.

I'm sick of eating the same thing over and over, she said. Not being able to go to restaurants, having to race in and out of the supermarket, trying not to attract attention, hiding all the time.

Do we have another option? he asked.

We could leave the country, she said. Can't you see the situation's getting worse by the day? How many friends of ours are in prison? At the meeting today, they mentioned a certain Humberto. Do you know him? From what I understood, if they catch him, he's dead, she said.

He fidgeted. Did you see where I put the ashtray?

I think it's in the living room.

Weak with terror, he left the kitchen to look for his cigarette, tripping over his own legs. She kept talking to him, talking to herself. She couldn't bear the clandestine lifestyle anymore; it wasn't the life she had dreamed of for herself.

She brought the plates of pasta on a tray. He had smoked another three cigarettes, one after another. His pallid face was sweaty. She didn't notice, engrossed in her idea to leave the country. With his head down, he whispered something that she didn't understand.

What?

He looked up and repeated himself: Sit here, next to me. They were living in a bedsit in the outskirts of town, a flat the party had arranged for them. Nothing in it was theirs except for their clothes. She felt her husband's cold hand holding hers like that of a boy frightened by a storm on a moonless night. She knew his heart was beating wildly, and hers sped up too.

What's wrong?

He didn't answer and bowed his head again.

What's wrong?

Stay calm, he said, please stay calm. I need to tell you something, but please don't hate me, don't be upset with me. I'll explain everything properly later, but right now all that matters is that you know, that you understand, that you accept that I've kept a secret from you all this time. Her silent eyes said what her voice couldn't, and when he whispered: My love, I'm Humberto, she had already put her head down and pressed her hands to her ears so she wouldn't have to hear what she had already understood.

Outside, a light rain was falling. I still had no idea what the city was like. The plane had been almost four hours late, and I'd spent more time waiting for it than in it. By the time I got to Smyrna it was already night, so I took a taxi to the hotel. The trip had tired me out. My body ached, my shoulders were stiff. I wasn't sure if it was the wait for the plane or being in a hurry to get to the end of this story that had installed pain in my body once again. In the airport lounge, it had occurred to me that simply not being able to go to Smyrna due to bad weather or something like that might be a fitting end. But I had eventually boarded the plane, and there I was, in the city my grandfather was from.

I was already in possession of a phone book (the receptionist had seemed surprised by my request, but she was also helpful, and had offered to show me how to look for what I needed). I had to be prepared, because if for some reason I didn't find either of the names I was looking for, I had no doubt that my body would seize up right then and there and go back to being the monolith it was before leaving Brazil. My room offered a few luxuries, and I made the most of what I could. A bath would do my rock-hard muscles good. I left the hot water running as I unpacked. When the tub was almost full, I lowered myself in, until my head sank under the almost scalding water. I felt my muscles melting like ice cubes in contact with water. I even heard my joints crack. There is nothing like relaxing in hot water. It was as if everything I had accumulated so far was working loose and sliding off me. I lost track of time as I lolled in the tub, barely thinking a thing, almost asleep, letting the water do what I couldn't.

It was only after I was dressed that I sat on the bed, back against the wall, with the phone book on my lap. I looked for the letter S — apart from a few differences, the Turkish alphabet is almost the same as ours — and, with my eyes following my index finger, I got closer and closer to my own surname. I took a deep breath, afraid my heart would leap out of my mouth. There it was, just like the name on my driver's licence. I looked for the names that my grandfather had given me and found three Raphaels and one Salomon. I jotted down their phone numbers and addresses. Were they the cousins I was looking for? A shiver ran through me and I wanted to climb back into the bathtub and never get out again. I looked at the clock: it was almost eleven, too late to go calling people I didn't know, in spite of the suspicion that we might belong to the same family. Better leave it for tomorrow, I told myself, as my eyes closed slowly, effortlessly.

~

When you leaned over to whisper sweetly in my ear, I was scared, very scared. I shook. Take off your clothes. Take off your clothes and wait for me on the bed, you ordered. Feeling trapped, I obeyed. That day I discovered that what we felt wasn't love.

~

First the unleavened bread, dry and flavourless, to remember the suffering of the expelled tribes wandering the desert. Then the apple with honey, so we won't go hungry or live in poverty, so we'll have a sweet year. I dip the slice of apple in the honey pot and cover it entirely. I want a really sweet year. I'm tired of chewing on flour and water. There aren't many of us around the table, perhaps seven. The bread is passed around and everyone takes a piece as they repeat: *el pan de la afriisyon ke komyeram nuestros padres em tyeras de Ayifto*. Then the apple: *Shanah Tovah!* There was nothing religious about the ritual. To me, there was always something missing. The truth. It was all a big enactment: we were Jewish for one day a year. We celebrated the New Year, but for us the year didn't begin until 1 January. The year never began in September or October. So why the celebration? Why pretend to ourselves? *I don't understand why you say there was no truth in it. God wasn't at the table, I agree; that was our choice. It wasn't religion that was important to us, but tradition. We didn't want to throw away everything our forebears had gone to such lengths to preserve. What mattered was maintaining the symbology. I wanted to pass on a little of what I learned to those who came after me.* I know. I understand your gesture; I understand your intention. Breaking ties with the past once and for all is harder than we think — the guilt can kill us. I think that's why we're Jews even when we're not. We say it's genealogy, but it's fear more than anything. We're afraid of forgetting the past and being responsible for it. *The past isn't to be forgotten.* If we don't forget the past we don't live in the present. You know, this pain I feel in my body, the weight on my shoulders, is the unforgotten past that I carry with me. The past of generations and generations. *No, my child, what you carry on your fragile shoulders are the silences of the past. You carry what has never been uttered, what has never been heard. I warned you, silence is dangerous.* But it isn't my fault, I wasn't the one who kept secrets. They came to me without my permission, and I don't even know what they are. *Yes, you do — your body knows all secrets, all silences, more than you can imagine.* So, you do believe it's an inheritance? That I've inherited all of the family's pain? Nice present! *Don't be upset, it's not worth it. Don't shirk your responsibility either. You are responsible for your past too. You are responsible for what you carry on your shoulders and, above all, how you carry it. There are different ways to deal with inheritance, and you have surely chosen one of the most difficult, the most painful.* I didn't choose a thing, I already told you. I came into the world with this burden. *I was there when you were born and I remember clearly — you were a cute, chubby baby, there was nothing heavy about your soft little body.* Don't be ironic. You know what I'm talking about. *I'm not being ironic. I just want you to try to see things as they are. I want you to believe in this journey, to believe that you deserve to be happy, that you can be. I want you to understand that you don't need to carry your family on your back, that you can be free of the past. But in order to do so you can't ignore it, for the simple reason that you haven't so far. You need to understand it and you need to name it.* I've already named it: the name of the past is fear. *I've never met anyone so stubborn. For each step forward, you seem to take one back. The name of the past isn't fear. Don't question things so much, my child, just carry on and you'll see the surprises that await you, you'll see how light life can be.* You tell me this now, but don't forget that it was you who taught me that before the sweet apple we must eat the dry bread. *That's right. The matzah serves as a reminder of the troubled past. The dry bread speaks of pain, of misery. And the apple with honey is so that we don't repeat the past.* If everyone talks about the past, why must I carry their silences? *I understand your concern. Many things haven't been said, and they are dragging you down. Fear has intercepted speech. But now it is up to you, it is up to those who remain, to tell the story, to retell it.*

It is up to you not to repeat the same mistakes. It is up to you to speak in the name of those who didn't.

I tell (make up) this story about my ancestors, this story of immigration and its losses, this story about the key to the house in Smyrna, about my hope of returning to the place that my forebears came from, but you and I (just the two of us) know that the real reason for my paralysis is something else. I tell (make up) this story to justify my immobility, to give the world and, in a way, myself, an answer, but you and I (just the two of us) know the truth. I wasn't born like this. I wasn't born in a wheelchair; I wasn't born old. There is no gust of ancient times at my back. I became like this. I lost my movements one by one after I met you. After I loved you, after I knew madness through love, our love. It was love (without boundaries) that slowly took away my movement, left me paralysed in this musty bed.

They were ready for bed when she announced categorically: I got us asylum at the Costa Rican embassy. He pretended he hadn't heard. She repeated herself: I got us asylum at the Costa Rican embassy. He kept pretending he hadn't heard. She said: I can't live in hiding anymore. Let's do as so many others have. We've held out more than most. We've been underground for four years. Don't you see there's no more hope for us here? When things improve (and one day they will, have faith) we'll come back. He climbed under the covers and lay down, still pretending he hadn't heard. Irritated, she said: Well, I'm not going to keep on talking to the walls. If you don't want to come with me, I'll go on my own.

A few days after you died, the doctor phoned to ask how our return to Brazil had gone, if everything was under control. No, I said, nothing's under control. There's nothing else anyone can do, not me, not you, not the best hospital in the world. He spluttered and then was quiet. I was afraid I was going to hear my verdict in his voice. I thought he was going to say that it was my fault, that I'd broken the rules by laying beside you in the hospital bed, that I hadn't worn a mask or gloves, that I hadn't doused the catheter with enough alcohol before injecting your medication (remember that when we left the hospital they trained me to be your private nurse?). I thought he was going to say that if I'd followed his instructions to a T you wouldn't have died. When I heard his silence, I was sure I was about to hear my verdict: guilty. But no, the words I heard were unexpected; they were sweet and caring. He had become involved, Mother. His doctor's carapace had given way to a compassionate man.

So I won't get confused, I write the things I should say on a piece of paper: who I am, where I'm from, why I'm calling, what I want. I start by calling Salomon, since there is only one in the phone book. The phone rings and rings, but no one answers. I call again. After several rings, a woman picks up. I ask if she speaks English. She hangs up. I wish I could just give up, not have to go through it all again. I take a deep breath, dial again, and the only thing I say is Salomon. She says something in Turkish and I don't understand a thing. I repeat: Salomon, and she continues speaking in this language that is completely alien to me. Once again I ask if she speaks English, and she hangs up again.

This isn't going to work, I think to myself. And in this wave of pessimism I think how naive I am, and wonder how I could have believed I might actually locate my relatives. I pick up the phone, but this time to call Brazil: Grandpa, I found the names in the phone book. I called Salomon's house, but a woman answered in Turkish. If I don't speak Turkish, how am I supposed to communicate with them? He starts to laugh, and I snap: What's so funny? Sweetly, he manages to turn my mood around, convincing me that these setbacks are part of the journey, that he never imagined it would be simple and that it isn't the end of the world: Stay calm, sugar plum, it's too early to admit defeat.

But how am I going to talk to them?

Try French. We all studied at French schools. And if that doesn't work, try Portuguese, or whatever you know of Spanish, because they're very similar to Ladino, which they still speak, no doubt.

Okay, I say, but I still have three different Raphaels to try.

See if one of them lives in Bornova, says my grandfather, and if so, try that one first.

None of them live there, so it's going to come down to luck. I choose the one in the middle and make the call with my fingers crossed, hoping it's the right one. A young man picks up and, to my relief, says he speaks French. I tell him I want to speak to Raphael, but when he says it is he, I suspect I have the wrong one. But I don't give up, and say: I'm from Brazil and I'm looking for my grandfather's cousin, who has the same name as you, but I don't have his number. I'm trying the Raphaels in the phone book. I found three, and you're the first one I've called.

He asks what my grandfather's name is. He sounds surprised. He wasn't expecting such an unusual call. My grandfather's name is Raphael too, he says, and he does have cousins in Brazil, who left many years ago. He offers to call his grandfather for me. I think it's a great idea — that way I won't have to start all over again. Give me the number where you are and I'll call you back as soon as I've spoken to him, he says.

When I hang up, I feel my body relax. I'm on the right track, I think. Finally, I repeat in silence and smile to myself.

No words hurt more than the absence of words. You weren't stupid and knew it very well. You'd impose devastating silences on me. You'd disappear and I wouldn't hear a peep out of you. You did it on purpose, to see me close to death, paralysed, sapped of strength. I'd wait for the phone the ring; it wouldn't. And if for some reason it did, it wasn't your voice on the other end. I'd wait for my computer to let me know a new email had arrived; it wouldn't. I'd wait for a letter, a text message, a smoke signal. I'd wait for you to show up, bringing words with you. I'd wait and wait and wait. But you never came. You'd leave me alone with this silence that hurts more than a piercing scream, than a deep cut to the flesh, than the word *pain* itself. I'd talk to myself, sing in the shower, call friends. I'd go crazy, desperate for a voice, for words. But yours never came, and the more time that passed, the harder I looked for them, the less hope I had of ever regaining my movement.

They carted her off to prison one afternoon when he wasn't around. Early in the evening, when no one answered the phone, he presumed the worst. He called the flat for days on end, and didn't return. She was kicking herself for not having left the country. Why had she given in? Out of love for him or for the homeland? But she wasn't furious. She was terrified, and the terror emanated from her eyes, her nostrils, the pores of her skin. She wished she could leave. Please let me go, sir. I have nothing to do with this story, I'm not who you think I am. I'm a nice girl from a respectable family. This is all a mistake. But where she was, such words meant nothing. The only valid words were the ones she didn't want to utter. And wouldn't.

I have a really big secret. So big that sometimes it grips my body and makes me repeat over and over: I can't take it anymore I can't take it anymore I can't take it anymore. Silence is dangerous, you always told me. This danger is present daily and I feel the discomfort of not being able to speak. I feel the secret corroding me, slowly mutilating me. It's a terrible, monstrous secret; there is nothing even remotely beautiful about it. It stinks more than sulphur, more than rotten food, more than a sick person's vomit. If I could hold it in my hands, it would be viscous as phlegm, as a secretion. It is an ugly, ugly secret. Which is why I decided not to tell you, because I didn't want you to suffer any more than you already had. But it was also out of fear. I once told another person this secret, and they said: You're brave not to tell your mother. But the truth is, I'm not brave, I'm fearful, and that's why I never told you. I still live with the danger of this silence. I carry, in my paralysed body, every word never uttered. Even now, Mother, with me here and you there, I don't have the courage to tell you. And yet I need to speak, I need to tell you the truth. But I'm afraid, very afraid, because I know how painful it will be, and I don't want to hurt you.

Do you remember how, when I was young, every time I wanted to tell you a secret (like my first period, my first kiss), instead of speaking, I'd write it on a piece of paper and leave it in your room for you to find? I was so afraid to speak, but at the same time I wanted you to know, I wanted to tell you. So I used a pen and paper. I know I'm a little old for this strategy now, and I also know that we were intimate enough for me to have looked you in the eye and told you. But I was afraid to see the fear and pain on your face and feel responsible for it. Since I can't think of any other way to tell you what I've kept secret for so long, I'll write you a letter to reveal what has brought me so much agony, the terrible secret that torments me to this day and makes me repeat over and over: I can't take it anymore I can't take it anymore I can't take it anymore. Then I'll find a park, a garden, or perhaps a forest, where I'll dig a hole and bury the secret. I'll put a little honey on the letter to disguise the bitter taste. I'll cover the envelope with earth and then I'll plant a rose bush. The rose bush will be the most beautiful in the park, the most showy. That way, Mother, when you find the letter, when you discover the secret and feel a knot in your heart, accept the roses that will be there as if they were a kiss from me, a small solace.

I'd wake up and before I even made a coffee, I'd turn on my computer and mobile phone. I'd check my email and voicemail for any sign of you. My thoughts had a single objective: you. Twenty-four hours a day, as I ate, as I worked, as I bathed, as I slept, all I could think about was you. After breakfast I'd head straight for the study. I'd read newspapers on the internet, a blog post or two by friends, and check my email again. I'd leave my mobile on the desk beside me. Then I'd start to write. I'd write a word and then another, and then I'd check my mobile again for messages or missed calls (I might not have heard it, it might not have rung — these things happen). I'd delete the two words on the screen and write another three. I'd get up and wander through the living room, through the kitchen. In my mind, a single thought: you. An obsession. I'd have a second coffee. I'd wander around the flat looking for inspiration, but all I'd find was you, in every corner, every idea. I'd go back to the study and start writing again. A few words would appear on the computer screen, and they'd all feel like the same one: you. I'd delete everything and check my email: advertising, friends inviting me out or asking favours, information on lectures and courses. From you: nothing, not a word, not a sign. Forget him, I'd repeat to myself. Focus on your work; write. I'd look at the screen again and see a blank page. I'd change the formatting: the spacing, the font. Sometimes it would work — I'd change the font and would manage, as if by a miracle, to write a whole paragraph in one sitting. Then I'd get up and wander through the living room and kitchen again. Third coffee. Study. Emails, mobile: nothing. Suddenly the phone would ring and I'd leap to answer it. It might be you. Telephone operators offering services,

Dad asking if everything was alright, Grandpa, the odd friend. The computer screen again, the inability to write. I'd go into the bedroom and lie on the still-unmade bed. Curtains closed, as if it were night. From under the blanket, I'd stare at the ceiling and ask myself if one day it would pass, if one day I'd stop thinking about you.

My nights are taken up with nightmares, and between them there is only a brief moment of fright, in which I wake up and realise I'm covered in sweat. Then I go back to sleep and have another nightmare. I'm in a house I don't know but I recognise many things: my grandfather's portrait on the wall, my grandmother's crystal glasses, the Turkish rugs from my apartment, black-and-white photographs, the table with the glass top, the musty smell of things kept in cupboards. The whole house is made of dark wood, the floor lined with handmade rugs. A flight of stairs leads to the second floor, and I don't know what is up there. It is the house I've spent my whole life in, the house I've never been in. I'm alone, and solitude frightens me. I've spent my life in this house and have been trying to leave it forever, in vain. The door is locked with a key, and I can't find it. The walls are solid: they must be made of stone. The door is large, heavy, as if it were composed of different layers. I hunt for the key incessantly, rummaging in the same places over and over: the same drawers, the same corners. I can't find it. I try to call for help, but I have no voice. I don't know what's outside — or even if there is something, or if I'm in an abandoned house in the middle of nowhere. I wish I were Alice in Wonderland so I could slip through the keyhole, see the other side of the world. I wish I could see the sky and the trees that must be out there. I wish I could meet someone and walk hand in hand through the night. I wish I could stroll through the garden that I imagine around the house and pick strawberries and collect them in my skirt. I wish I could walk away from the house, see what I have never seen, never experienced. But the door is closed and there are no windows. My body wastes away; my story is intertwined with the walls and the death that awaits me.

Pain is in everything. It is in every corner of the globe, every corner of ourselves. There isn't a pore of our skin that is free from it. Feelings change, but pain persists. In everything I have experienced, there it was, one way or another. In love, in happiness, in sadness, in suffering, in mourning, in dreams — I never knew any of it without pain. I don't agree when you say that I always focus on pain. It isn't me, Mother, it's life; life is like that.

This journey I am undertaking, this strange country I find myself in, it all hurts. It's beautiful, it's interesting, it's funny, but it hurts. This inheritance hurts. The things I bring with me without choosing to hurt. This conversation of ours, Mother, hurts too. The love story that exacted a pound of my flesh hurts. Grandpa's story, your story, your torture, our exile; it all hurts. And, above all, it hurts to talk about the hurting. It hurts to write this story. Every new word I find hurts. Writing, Mother, hurts immensely. It hurts as much as it has to.

We hadn't seen each other for over a month. You called me and said, I need to see you. I didn't want to, but I needed to too, I wanted to too. When I heard the doorbell, I felt as if a date had arrived. I wanted to escape through the window but couldn't. I shuddered with fear, terror, desire, nostalgia. Come in, I called, the door's open. I was in the living room, sitting on the sofa. When I saw you, I stood up like an animal in danger, wary. You walked toward me and said: I miss you. You knew how to disarm me. I was still an animal in danger, but I no longer had the means to defend myself. I was shaking on the inside; my blood was racing. On the outside, I was just a defenceless girl. Your body was close to mine, almost flush against it; I registered your breathing, your smell, your presence, but I couldn't move. You look lovely, I heard. That was the second blow. The third was to unbutton my blouse. In my eyes were tears that didn't spill over. At that precise moment everything was extreme. Desire-elation-pleasure-pain: all together, all jumbled, all just one enormous thing, all immense, every emotion pulsing through my veins, through my paralysed body. You took off my blouse and let it fall to the ground. You unbuttoned my jeans, took them off, and dropped them on the ground too. Finally you pulled off my knickers and left me without anything on. It was as if you were touching my organs directly, my blood, my flesh, without any protection. That's how it felt when you ran your hands over my breasts over my stomach over my thighs between my thighs, when you stroked my face and lightly tugged on my hair, when you ran your lips over my entire body, when you took me, when you squeezed my legs, when you made me wet and I wet you too. That's how it felt from beginning to end: you touched my skin and I had no skin.

In a room that was three metres square, they turned on the air conditioner and set it to the lowest temperature. They wanted to make the place into a refrigerator. It was the first time she had experienced such harsh cold. She felt the skin of her face begin to crack, her naked body ready to splinter like ice. She shook. Her teeth chattered. She sensed the end was near and regretted getting involved; she didn't want to die. Immediately afterwards she didn't regret it: if she died, it would be for the right cause. She shook so much that it felt like her arms wanted to flee her body. She began to do star jumps, without stopping. For almost two hours she exercised, until she didn't feel quite as cold. Warmer now, she sat down to rest. Then the cold began to ease off. She realised that the air conditioner wasn't even on anymore. Were they going to take her out of there? Her heartbeat quickened. No one could have imagined how badly she yearned to see the daylight. She was filled with hope: she would see her husband again, her parents, her friends. She promised herself that from then on she wouldn't put her life at risk, not hers or her family's. Her father had always said: Did I give you the best money could buy for *this*? So you could put everything on the line? Was that why you got married? How are you going to give me grandchildren like this?

But it's for them that I am doing this, for the children I'll have one day, she had replied.

She felt the moment was arriving, that soon she'd be reunited with her loved ones, taken out of the room, delivered home. Suddenly her neck felt hot. She was perspiring. Her forehead was moist. Droplets of sweat began to trickle down her body. The heat was intensifying, becoming oppressive. No, she wasn't going to get out of there. With the thermostat turned up as high as possible, the room was now an oven.

If someone had asked, I'd have said I'd never thought about travelling in search of the past. I had always believed that there was nothing to be gained by poking around in the ruins of things that no longer existed; that memories were the vestiges of tears that had dried on the faces of those who had departed. Now, leaving the hotel after having found a clue that might lead me to my family, it occurred to me that the tears were not just mine, and, contrary to what I had imagined, they still weren't dry.

From what they had told me at the hotel, Smyrna was a small city with a few tourist attractions, but nothing comparable to Istanbul. There might not have been any great monuments to see, but every last nook and cranny of the city — every door, house, and person — left me with a lump in my throat. I could have been born there and it could have been my city. I strolled around the port, along Atatürk Caddesi, and it occurred to me that it must have been right there that my grandfather had boarded the steamer to Brazil. Thc huge ship he had told me about had sailed this sea, docked in these same waters. The city must have been very different, I imagined, without the cars that now clogged the streets with traffic, without so many buildings, so much urbanisation. I thought that, in fact, this wasn't my grandfather's city; cities, like ourselves, have their own memories, their own vestiges of tears.

The face of Smyrna struck me as drier than my own. The hot sun — not as hot as in Istanbul — beat down on Konak Square, where the clock tower stood. I lay on the wall separating the asphalt from the sea and ended up dozing off. I only woke up when a girl poked me to ask if I wanted to buy a box of raisins. I was hungry, so I took her up on her offer. Behind the clock was a city that I had yet to see, but which I could almost divine in its designs, its smells, its colours.

I sat in a nearby café and ordered a cup of apple tea. I didn't feel like exploring the city right then. I preferred to sit staring at the sea and imagining what it must have been like to leave. Then I wondered if Raphael's grandfather really was my grandfather's cousin, and if I was ever going to meet him, talk to him. This was the city I was looking for — not the city of the carpets and gold, not the city of tobacco and good food, but my family's city.

Tell me when you're about to come.

We both smelled freshly showered. My hair was still wet; yours, almost dry. Your body on top of mine, in the most obvious, but indispensable, position. Our towels were lying next to us, making the sheets damp. It was a Saturday morning, and the shower had been an attempt to cure ourselves of a hangover after a Friday night that had gone on into the small hours.

I'm almost there.

Wait a minute, I murmured in your ear. You slowly withdrew and, starting with my lips, kissed me all over. The night before we had celebrated our second anniversary together. (Who'd have imagined we'd be together for so long? was the gem you offered me over dinner.) Mushroom risotto with plenty of champagne. For dessert, petit gâteau with guava paste and cheese-flavoured ice cream. Come back, I said. Come on top, you said. I smiled. You knew how much I liked having you underneath me, doing things my way, at my pace. I slotted us together slowly, with morning laziness, in an attempt to stretch out the time that we didn't want to pass. I ran my hands over your almost-smooth, almost-white chest, the redness of summer having faded.

Come, you said, I want to come with you.

Then wait, I said in a voice that made it clear you wouldn't have to wait long. Just a bit longer.

After dinner we had gone out to dance, which we hadn't done for quite some time. A real nightclub, with electronic music. The dancefloor was packed with women in miniskirts or tight jeans, tops showing off belly-button piercings; men with the top buttons of their shirts undone, gel in their hair; caipirinhas and beer spilled on the ground, on clothes. There we were, as if we did it all the time, dancing all night, rubbing our bodies against each other and against other people, kissing with our tongues out, displaying our lust in public. I'm almost there, I said, and you took one hand off my hip and pressed it to my clitoris. I bit my lip and closed my eyes tightly. I thought about our sweaty bodies dancing, your large, muscular body as you unabashedly pressed yourself against me from behind and squeezed my waist, trying to fondle my indiscreet breasts without anyone noticing. I'm coming, you said, and it made me come, you come, our spasms together. Afterwards we didn't say anything else, didn't think anything, didn't want anything.

Breathe: quickly, before they dunk you again. Hang in there, you can take it. There were three men, three brutes, standing over her. She was no longer a woman, just a gaunt, debilitated body, loose skin trying to hold together bones. Every time they plunged her head into the basin, her legs would buckle under her. Then, to stop her from falling, one of the torturers would press down harder on her head to compensate for the lack of support from her legs. She heard distorted voices through the water but even if she'd had the strength to make an effort she wouldn't have been able to understand what they were saying. Breathe: quickly, before they dunk you again. Hang in there, you can take it. She didn't think about anything specific. Images floated up, diffuse and without explanation. She had heard that before you die your life passes before your eyes like in a film, frame by frame. Was that it? Was she dying? Were these her last images? She didn't react and merely let it happen. When they lifted her head up, she had no time — or intention — to speak, to ask them to stop because she was going to tell them what they wanted to hear. Breathe: quickly, before they dunk you again. Hang in there, you can take it. They repeated the same movement dozens of times: head in water, head up. Until they saw that her eyes were closed and her body limp, and they stopped. They dumped her on the cold floor for an orderly to drag to her cell, where she would wait to be summoned again.

We were in the car and it was a long drive. Raphael asked if I'd enjoyed the dinner and apologised for his relatives. Politely, I said it had been great; there was no problem at all. As he drove, I studied his gestures, the outline of his face, the way he spoke. I thought that I could have been him, that it could have been me in his place. If I'd been born there I'd definitely be a real Jew — I'd speak their language, marry a Jew. If I'd been born there I wouldn't have found myself with my back against a wall. What, you don't speak our language? I had been caught off guard. They had all stared at me with incredulous, recriminating expressions on their faces, as if I'd committed a serious, if not grievous, offence. I'd listened to them talking among themselves in the language that I didn't speak. In front of me, Raphael had fidgeted and shot me sympathetic looks, as if thinking that it could have been him, that he could have been born in another country and not be able speak his grandparents' language. I found support in his eyes, trying hard to remain oblivious to what the others were saying, even though I was able to understand the odd word here and there. At some point, I had tried to justify myself. It was a question of survival, I said. My grandfather needed to forget the past, which is why he never taught anyone his language.

A real Jew doesn't forget the past, Raphael's grandfather had stated firmly. Maybe my grandfather wasn't a real Jew, I thought, but didn't say anything.

You know what the older generations are like, Raphael said when he pulled up at a red light. They don't mean to be like that. They're just afraid.

Yeah, I replied, that must be it. And I wondered if it was fear his grandfather had felt when he'd announced that only Ladino would be spoken during dinner and that all other languages were forbidden. No one had protested. Not Raphael; or Grandfather Raphael's wife, Judith; or Salomon's widow, Marta. I had wanted to run away, to shout in Portuguese that I had no reason to be there. Instead, I'd accepted the decision, smiled, and said in a mishmash of Portuguese and Spanish that I'd try. Despite this initial incident, I had noticed certain affinities. When I said that we made that same food at home, Grandfather Raphael had relaxed a little and smiled for the first time, as if thinking that the culture didn't reside in the language alone.

We were already in front of the hotel when Raphael asked if I wanted to go to Bornova the next day to see the neighbourhood where my forefathers used to live.

Apparently, he said, when your great-grandmother moved to Brazil, she left the house empty. It was abandoned for many years and demolished about fifteen years ago, but there are others very similar to it, built in the same era, in the same style.

I took the key out of my bag and stared at it, thinking that if the house wasn't there anymore, I had no reason to go. I didn't say a word, but he understood. I wondered if we'd ever see each other again and perhaps he was thinking the same thing. His nose was narrow, like mine, but we were very different. I'd never have imagined we were cousins. He smiled, and I suddenly felt an urge to kiss him. I felt an urge to kiss him repeatedly, to put my arms around him, invite him up to my room, spend the night with him. But we said goodbye with simple pecks on the cheek, saying that we hoped to see each other again soon. I closed the car door and, as I headed up to my room, it occurred to me that I had nothing left to do in this country. I'm not sure I ever did.

Angrily, hatefully, I hurl the typewriter to the ground and tear up everything I have written. I tear up the blank pages too, so there is no risk that I might keep on writing. I realise how useless it is to write this journey back to my origins. I don't want to write another word. I want to destroy what has already been committed to paper. This journey has no reason to exist, in reality or on the page.

Sometimes we'd stay at home all weekend. You knew how to touch me like no man. You made me come like no man. You made me believe it was love. I believed that I loved you. I believed that you loved me. On days like that, I'd simply forget that I was covered in wounds, that you'd flayed my skin. On days like that, I'd pretend my body was whole and I'd offer it up to you. You knew how to touch it without hurting me, without your hands coming into contact with my wounds. You forgot too and you pretended too. To this day, I don't know if there was love in that madness, but I try to convince myself that there wasn't, that it can't have been love. I try to believe that love is something else, that it doesn't lay waste to the body like that, it doesn't flay your skin or leave you so vulnerable, flesh exposed. I try to believe it, but I'm afraid I might be wrong. To be honest, I'm terrified that love is this invasive pain that devours the body, the soul.

They all laid their forks on their plates and looked in my direction when I asked: Is my grandfather's house still standing? Raphael hesitated and then looked up and said: No, did you want to see it? I told him that my grandfather had given me the key to try and open the door of his former home. He gave me a quizzical look. Doesn't your grandfather know the house was demolished?

he asked. Taken by surprise, I stammered: I don't think so. But it got me wondering.

He didn't get up to answer the door; in fact, the sound barely registered with him. He had long since given up checking to see who was there when the doorbell rang. When he was finally convinced there was nothing he could do, he gave in to despondency. He only went out to buy what was absolutely essential in order to survive. He felt too guilty to just pick up where he'd left off. He never should have left her on her own. Why hadn't he gone with her? Why hadn't he listened to her endless pleas to seek exile at the Costa Rican embassy? The choice to fight had been his, not hers. He felt responsible.

The doorbell kept ringing, but the intervals between one ring and another were too long. It sounded like a lament, the last request of someone without strength. Only then, after almost an hour, did he sense that … Yes, it was her on the other side of the door, dressed in the clothes she had been wearing the day they took her — the same pair of jeans, the same grey t-shirt, the same leather bag slung across her body. But what about the rest of her? What had they done with her eyes? With her smile? It was her, crouching on the doorstep, head between her knees.

Her. He was still standing. It took some effort to carry her to the sofa in his equally weak arms. He set her down carefully and stretched out beside her. He couldn't stop crying. She just lay there, unspeaking. They lost track of time lying there like that: he in tears and she inert, expressionless. It might have been a day or two, or months, years; it might have been forever. Without exchanging a word, arms around each other, feeling the same pain, but such different pain.

I'm pregnant, I said.

Get rid of it, you said without flinching.

Get rid of it? No way.

What do you mean, no way? Do you think I'm going to have a kid at this point in my life?

I don't think so, I said. I know so.

Oh no I'm not, you insisted.

Oh yes you are, I said, holding my ground.

We'll see, you said.

And we didn't broach the subject again, each of us firm in our certainty.

A week later I understood how contradictory our wishes were. To this day I don't know if it was you or my fear. We were having breakfast together, as usual, when I felt a twinge in my abdomen, like a period cramp, but sharper. Clutching my stomach, I doubled over. You acted worried, and came over to put your arm around me. What is it?

I didn't answer. I just howled in agony and pushed you away. I was angry. In my heart there was only room for hatred and the certainty that it was you. Then, with my head between my legs, I saw blood come gushing out of me, spreading over my legs, running down the chair. Without looking up, I cried out for the child I had lost, the child I already loved. Not for a second in the hours to come — not even when I was in the hospital, recomposed, out of danger — did I raise my head, not for a second did I look you in the eye. I was afraid to find the answer I wanted to avoid, to discover a terrible confession. I was afraid you didn't know how to lie well enough to hide the truth from me.

Between dessert and tea, Raphael asked: Why didn't your grandfather come to try and open the door himself?

I have the same dream over and over. I am asleep and you arrive and sit on the bed next to me. You stroke my hair in silence. I wake up and see you. Before I have time to be surprised, you say, I'm back. Staring into my eyes, you say, I had to go away, but I'm back now. I squeeze your hand tightly so you won't escape me this time. Then I frown and ask: You mean, you had a choice?

I was alone again, wandering the city. I thought about everything I'd done so far. The dinner with the family was still drifting through my thoughts, in a mixture of disappointment, contentment, and amusement. As I strolled through the streets of Smyrna, I felt that I'd already completed the first part of my journey. I didn't have anything else to do in Turkey and I still wanted to go to Portugal, where there were neither relatives nor a house to look for. Nevertheless, it was my family's country of origin and the place I was born. I was nine months old when I left, in my mother's arms. Not enough time in which to form memories, to be sure, but even so I believed I might find some meaning in Lisbon for my body, my story.

They had spent almost a month at the consulate without contact with the outside world, unable to leave, to make phone calls, receive visitors, anything. It was the eve of their departure for Costa Rica. The vice consul knocked on the door of the room they slept in. You know visits are not allowed, but she insisted. She decided to take the risk and come to see you. She says she can't let her daughter leave without saying goodbye first. I'm going to allow it because you're leaving the country tomorrow, and we don't know for how long, but be brief. No more than fifteen minutes.

She looked at her husband with tears in her eyes. My mother's here. Good God, she's crazy. She tidied her hair and went to see her. Fifteen minutes — no longer, repeated the vice consul.

They hadn't seen each other for over a year. They had spoken a few times by telephone, when she had managed to get to a public phone booth. But it was always in a hurry, and their conversations were strange, almost in code, with no names or places, just to say: I'm fine, don't worry, everything will be okay. On the other end, her mother's fretful voice, on the verge of tears: Don't stay here, honey, leave the country.

There she was, hunched over like a hook. The hall was large and she ran to get to her as quickly as possible. Her mother was shorter than her and fit into her embrace like a child. They cried without speaking, just hugging each other and sobbing. Nothing they could have said, no word they could have uttered, would have scratched the surface of everything they had to say to each other. How much they missed each other, the lumps in their throats, the clandestine life of one, the quiet life of the other, their plans, projects, home, lack of home. Do you know the risk you're taking to come here? She didn't answer. Of course she knew, but how could you weigh up the risk? How could she not see her daughter? The day she had children of her own, she'd understand.

Does Dad know?

No, he wouldn't have let me come. She shook her head, as if reprimanding a naughty child. They touched each other, a confusion of hands, faces, and caresses. I miss you so much, darling; I miss you so much, Mother.

They sat on the sofa. Her mother was getting old. Her stout legs, purple with varicose veins, couldn't stand for too long. She tired easily and had many health problems — so many doctors, medications, pills with each meal.

How are you, darling?

I'm fine. We leave tomorrow. We won't have to hide anymore.

I'm relieved.

You'll come to visit us as soon as you can, won't you?

Of course we will, your father and I. Call us, write, send news. We'll be on the first plane.

She smiled and breathed easier, relaxing. There, in that hall, on that sofa, she left behind her fear, her anxiety, and the pain of separation. Although they were about to part, this time her heart was filled with the certainty that she'd see her mother again. And every certainty that came to her was a fear that left her. The vice consul came to the door: Your time's up.

They looked at each other tenderly, not ready to say goodbye yet. Fifteen minutes were nothing after more than a year of distance. She stood, went over to the austere gentleman waiting stiffly for her at the door, and said: What difference does it make if she stays fifteen minutes or an hour? She's already here, nothing else can happen. We haven't seen each other for a long time, and we still don't know how long it will be before we see each other again. I could argue that we're mother and daughter, and we have so much to say to each other, but all I ask is: what difference does it make?

He frowned, and didn't speak for a few seconds. Fine, you can have a little longer, but I'll be back in forty-five minutes. And then I'll have to ask your mother to leave.

They hugged again and now they began to talk, telling each other everything they hadn't in the last fifteen minutes. Her mother told her about her brother and sisters, the grandchildren that had been born, her dad and his business, the work they'd had done to the house because of a leak, her tiredness, but also her walks along the beachfront, how she liked to watch the sun set in Leblon and get out and about when her body let her. She, on the other hand, didn't have a whole lot of news. Most of all, she talked about the tension, the fear, and the places they hid, but she hoped her situation would improve from there on. Her mother knew she had been taken prisoner, but she didn't know (or want to know?) what had happened in there. It was too much for her motherly heart, her fragile body. One day the daughter would tell her everything, because she believed that pain should be voiced, that silence was dangerous. She'd tell her everything that took place while she was locked up, but not today, not on this day of reunions and goodbyes, not after so long without seeing each other. She didn't want to worry her mother unnecessarily. She'd wait for the right moment, when she was in exile — no longer in Costa Rica but in Portugal. When her mother went to visit her and they had time, lots of time, to themselves — not the time on the watch of the vice consul, the gentleman who returned punctually to say their hour was up, he'd been too lenient already. The time had come, they'd have to part and say their goodbyes, but not to worry, as it wouldn't be long before they'd be able to see each other again. When he finished speaking he lowered his head, knowing they'd be giving each other a parting embrace, hugging tightly, stroking each other's faces lovingly, and crying because they already missed each other, as mothers and daughters do when they have to say goodbye.

There was no love between us. There was fear.

When you left, it was as if I'd known from the beginning. Yes, you can say that everyone knows, we all know, death is our only certainty. But there is something beyond this certainty, an even bigger certainty, greater than the certainty of death. And that was where my fear came from. When you died, it was a confirmation, as if death had been lying in wait for us the whole time, watching our every move. When it came, I knew it had to be like that; I'd always known, from the outset. But knowing it hadn't brought me any peace. On the contrary, it brought me the deepest fear, the most acute outrage, agonising discomfort.

I want to scream, but my mouth is gagged. My body lying on the bed in this foul, lonely room is a body in silence.

I doubt there is a person alive who has never felt the urge to kill someone. Perhaps few have felt it as intensely as I have, it is true, but I imagine that at least once in life everyone feels the macabre desire to see the fear of death in someone else's eyes. I hatched plots during my nights of insomnia. I didn't just want you to die — I wanted to be the one to kill you. I wanted to see the desperation in your eyes when you realised you were going to die by my hand. Like in a film or a book. Like in one of those cheap newspapers that are available every morning, whose cover story is a bizarre murder: a son who killed his mother, or a husband who killed his wife after catching her in bed with another man. I wanted to be the one in the news the next day: Young Woman Kills Boyfriend During Fight. All planned — the fight, the place, the weapon, the motive (self-defence: he killed me first). Sometimes I'd stare at your sleeping body, your snoring keeping me awake, the air blasting its way out of your mouth, and I'd wonder what it was like to perforate someone's stomach, to see their blood spurt out, their life escaping, slipping through my fingers. Sometimes hours would pass and I'd still be staring at you. Sometimes you'd wake up and ask: What's wrong?

Nothing, I just can't sleep.

Then you'd pull me to you and press your body to mine, side on, legs entwined, and kiss my neck. You'd softly whisper words that I barely understood and fall back asleep. Huddled there in your arms, I'd continue plotting, just waiting for the first light of day.

I went to Portugal to discover my origins and what I discovered was something else: don't be afraid of the word love. He told me this with his green eyes almost scorching mine. He said the word even though he knew he didn't love me (not yet), and love rang out in the room, echoing. I wanted to catch the sentence, trap its sounds in my arms. I don't know if I've ever been afraid of love, but the word, at large in the room like that, had never sounded so sweet. Don't be afraid of the word love.

No. I'm not.

How cruel (and beautiful) that life goes on after you.

It was Saturday night, and the music was playing at full volume. I was dancing in my underwear as Linda Scott sang, *I've told every little star*. A beer in my hand and several empty cans on the table. Dancing is like having sex, I had said before putting on the music. You pretended not to hear me. You didn't like to dance. You left me alone in the living room when I turned up the volume. That's okay, I thought. Few things are better on a Saturday night than beer, music, and being alone. Go do something else, it's fine by me. I danced and didn't think about it. I didn't think about anything. I smiled and smiled and danced and smiled. I swayed from side to side, my hand resting lightly on my hip.

It wasn't long before you were back. You couldn't handle being alone when I was fine with it. You appeared in the hall with your usual sarcastic smile, holding a beer and a cigarette in one hand and a CD in the other. You turned off my music and said: I'm going to put on that song you love. I nodded, smiling, liking the idea, not knowing yet what song it was. You came over and stroked my neck, brushing back my long hair, and then you kissed me and pressed the cold can to my breasts and tipped a little beer on my breasts and sucked my nipples and asked: So dancing is like having sex, is it?

I laughed, a drunken, light-hearted, happy laugh.

Is it? Is dancing like having sex?

I laughed again.

You tipped your cold beer over me and pulled away. Then I heard the song, our song. *My baby shot me down.* You had that look in your eye that terrified me. *Bang, bang.* You took aim and fired. You didn't even need a gun. You fired and fired and fired and your hands were free. You shot me down and I couldn't dance anymore, I couldn't move anymore. You left me alone again, and I didn't even know why. Lying on the ground until morning, I cried, mourning my own death.

He didn't know anything. He didn't know what I was doing in Lisbon, why I was there. When we met I still had my suitcase with me, and all he knew was that I had just arrived. And he thought that was all. That there was nothing before or after. I was at the A Brasileira. I had just had a coffee and decided to ask a passer-by to take a photo of me next to the statue of Fernando Pessoa. He was walking past with his hands free, so I said: Excuse me, would you mind taking a photo of me? He smiled, as I would too if someone asked me to take a photo of them in front of Sugarloaf Mountain in Rio. He didn't say anything and just took the photo. Then he wanted to make sure it had turned out okay. I took the camera and said: See, you just turn this dial.

What do you think? he asked.

Hmm, would you mind taking another one?

He smiled and nodded. I invited him to join me if he had time.

Sure, but why don't we go someplace else?

It was my turn to smile. Okay, why not? But would you mind if we didn't go very far? It's just that I've got my suitcase with me and it's a bit heavy.

We continued the smiling game, each grinning at what the other one was saying, as if we were both exotic creatures with funny accents, but also as if we understood each other perfectly and knew what the other one wanted.

The bar wasn't terribly close, but at least I didn't have to carry my suitcase. (I'll get that, he said politely.) It was certainly less touristy and, perhaps for that reason, cosier. We had nothing to talk about; we could have talked about everything, or anything. We had our whole lives to tell, but none of it seemed to matter very much, as if everything or nothing were the same. We ordered two Imperials and just drank them. And looked at each other. The silence between us grew until it was enormous, almost absolute, interrupted only by the occasional sound of us swallowing beer or blinking. When silence grows unchecked, when it is really big like that, it is even more dangerous. And that was what happened between us: the silence kept getting bigger and bigger, and so did the danger. The silence had been there for so long that if we spoke we'd have lost everything we'd created, as if a single word could make us ugly and uninteresting. We didn't hear the people shouting beside us, the men walking in and out, the women laughing too loudly, the young man arguing with the waiter because his sandwich wasn't the way he wanted it. We didn't hear the waiter asking us if everything was okay, or the glass falling off his tray and breaking on the floor. It was as if the world around us wasn't the world, as if the world was merely what existed between us. We didn't know anything about each other besides silence and stares, and, for that reason, there was no modesty, no shyness, no fear — there was just desire, silence, and danger, when we kissed for the first time.

Amnesty was granted in August 1979. One month later, she disembarked at Galeão International Airport with a dozen other political exiles. Photographers from most of Rio's newspapers and magazines were there to capture the euphoria of those arriving and the people who were there to greet them. The baby she was carrying wasn't bothered by the crowd, or frightened by the number of people who wanted to hold it. It seemed to recognise the home it hadn't seen before. When the Amnesty Law was passed, she had said: We don't need to go back right now, we're fine here in Portugal. The magazine likes my work as a correspondent and you've made contacts in the party all over the world. And our daughter is so small — it's too early to travel by plane, to change environments. But he had insisted: Our place is there. And it is there that I want to make the revolution.

He ended up convincing her that it was time to return. They hadn't seen family and friends, eaten cheese buns, or drunk caipirinhas for a long time.

It wasn't easy to pack. After all, they had been in exile for five years. They had to give away many things: paintings, sofas, their oven, their fridge. Many others — rugs, books, ceramics — they sent by ship. Their clothes went with them on the plane. She went ahead with the baby, while he stayed on for another two months to take care of paperwork and fulfil some party obligations. Before she left, she called her closest friends together and told them that, while she was happy she was going to see her loved ones after so long, she was sad to be leaving her Portuguese friends behind. There was one to whom she was especially close (they had met in Albania, where, at a party dinner, they had looked at each other and smiled when they saw a fly land in the leader's soup as he delivered a long, pompous speech) and whom she knew she'd miss tremendously. Their daughters were almost the same age, and it hurt to think that they wouldn't grow up together, as the mothers had so often imagined.

As she disembarked, a shiver raced up her spine and her heart beat faster. Who would be there to greet her? The wait for her luggage seemed interminable, even though she was chatting with an acquaintance she had bumped into in the arrivals area. She wanted to get out of there quickly, to really arrive. When she noticed the glass dividing wall she walked over, her bold olive eyes searching for a familiar face. She was surprised to see her father coming towards her, trailing his hand lightly over the glass. It had been so long! She would have said he was exactly the same, if he weren't a little more wrinkled and stooped than the last time they had seen each other. Their eyes glistened, but no tears fell. Imitating his gesture, she placed her hand against the glass as if she were holding his, and it was as though the glass didn't exist; they could even feel the heat of each other's hands. Suddenly he pointed at his granddaughter, noticing her for the first time. She looked from one to the other, from her father to her daughter, thinking things that were too obvious, too simple, things that reassured her that returning had been the best choice.

She felt a hand touch her shoulder. The acquaintance had come to say goodbye: I think your suitcases might have arrived. She was disconcerted. Oh, great, she said. I'll go take a look. And they wished each other good luck, all the best. As she pulled her bags off the carousel, she couldn't think about anything else: she wanted to rush out and hug her father, unfazed by the tumult that awaited her, the flashing cameras, the friends wanting to know how she was, her daughter being passed around. All she wanted was to feel that she had arrived.

You won't believe where I went today. *Where?* Strolling through Rossio Square, I suddenly saw, in large red letters, the name Pastelaria Suíça. *You're kidding! You went to Pastelaria Suíça?* Yes, you used to talk so much about their cakes and sweets that I never forgot the name. I couldn't believe it when I happened across the large al fresco area, with waiters walking back and forth holding trays piled high with goodies. *I used to love to sit at one of those tables and have a nice strong cup of coffee with something sweet. I'd pick a different one each day.* This is it! I thought. This is the place my mother always used to talk about. *How could I not? I remember as if it were yesterday: your grandmother had died in October 1977. In June 1978, on a sunny spring morning, Rossio Square brimming with people, I nervously walked into Estácio pharmacy to pick up the result of a pregnancy test.* Positive, *it read.* You're pregnant! *announced the little piece of paper. I jumped up and down, laughed to myself, beside myself. The square had never looked so beautiful. It was life's reply. I went to celebrate at the Pastelaria, where I ate until I had no more room.* That's exactly what I did. I sat at an outdoor table, with all the clamour of the square around me, the tourists, people out for a stroll or hurrying along for whatever reason. And I ordered two pastries: one for me and one for you.

I don't know if we were ever on the same wavelength, if there was a moment when we could state that we loved each other as a joyous truth, or if we just wandered through each other's lives like the vague characters of a certain Chinese filmmaker who portrays love as an impossibility. Every time I see his films I think about us, our impossible love, our love that went unrealised despite the years we spent together. I wonder if it could have been any different, or if the strength of our love lay precisely in its impossibility. All the times we embraced and I felt in my heart the painful certainty that you weren't mine. All the times we made love and I felt that it wasn't to each other, and that the distance between us wasn't a gap but an abyss. As if I was trying to hold your hand but you had no hand, as if I wanted to tell you I loved you but you had no ears. Although we lived under the same roof, shared the same bed, and did so very many things together, it was as if there was a knife with points at both ends wedged between us, and in order for us to get any closer we'd have to skewer ourselves simultaneously in the only possible embrace: of a blood-stained death.

I asked where his white horse was, but he said he didn't have one.

What about princely clothes?

I don't have any either.

A princely name?

Nope.

Well, do you have a bouquet of flowers?

I don't. But that's easy to fix — just a minute.

When he returned, he was holding a sweet-smelling bouquet of colourful wildflowers. With both hands behind his back, he said: Pick one.

Left, I said.

And, holding out his right hand, he said: Here, these are for you.

The flowers were beautiful. I smiled. I smiled a lot, sincerely. He took the bouquet from my hand and placed it carefully on the ground. Then we kissed. A tender kiss. We left holding hands, knowing that we weren't eternal, that we weren't prince and princess, but that our lips understood each other, that our mouths pressed lightly together was, perhaps, love.

I know you'll understand me. You've always been by my side and you know me well. We have come this far, hand in hand, and mine are moist with your sweat. We'll do everything with calm, great calm. Now it's my turn to tell you: don't be afraid. I stroke your face with my free hand. I feel you squeezing the other one. Don't be afraid, I repeat. You don't say a word. Your eyes fill with tears, as eyes typically do when one says goodbye. We are in the bedroom, and I can't stop looking at you. I don't want to forget a thing, not a single detail, although I know that one day I will — one day I will no longer be able to recall with precision the size of your nose, the shape of your mouth, the thickness of your hair. I know that one day I'll need a photograph to remind me of the small things. I thank you one last time and promise to keep your memory alive. My eyes are tearing up too. But I am no longer afraid. Gently, I pull your hand away from mine, and feel a little relieved when they part. Wait, I say. Even more gently, I take the ring off your finger and place it on mine. You smile, approving of my gesture. I tell you I'll take care of it, just as you once took care of me. Your smile grows broader. I take you in my arms and, together, we slowly lie down on the bed. I make you comfortable and run my hand over your hair, your face. I pass my hand over your eyes and you understand, you close them. I give you a big kiss for the last time. Then I take the two tips of the sheet bunched up at the foot of the bed and pull it over you, covering you entirely, like a burial shroud.

I don't know how many glasses of wine we had drunk. We had been naked for hours, sprawled across the floor, the bed, the sofa. Talking about unimportant things, very important things. Touching each other softly, without any hurry. We both knew the eternity of the hours that passed. I asked him: So, are you going to come live in Rio or am I coming to Lisbon? And we both laughed, a lot. We hooted with laughter. We also knew the brevity of time, which allowed us to play like two children, teenagers who make plans even when they're sure they'll never come to fruition.

I know, he said: Let's spend a week in each city. Every Sunday night, we'll go to the airport and change continents. That way we don't have to get rid of anything and we both keep our homes. I think it's the fairest thing to do.

And the most fun, I added.

We laughed again and drank more wine and kissed and made more plans and found each other more and lost each other more. I was so happy that I felt a knot forming in my heart, a pain I didn't know existed in the realm of happiness.

I need to talk to you, I said.

Okay, you said.

Come here, what I have to say is serious.

You sat down next to me on the sofa. I held your hand and blurted out everything that I had been planning and memorising for over a week. I talked without stopping, without a single pause in which you could interrupt me. You know how much I love you how important you are to me everything you've taught me everything I've learned from you you know I fell in love with you the minute we set eyes on each other you know better than anyone that no man before you has ever given me so much pleasure you know how much I admire and respect the beautiful person that you are you know you can always count on me because you're so special to me and always will be you know there will always be a place for you in my heart you know all this you know the depth of my feelings for you my love for you and that's why I think you'll understand of course you'll understand you must be thinking the same thing you must agree with me mustn't you my love you must think too that in spite of all the love we feel for each other unfortunately we can't go on we'll never be happy perhaps because our love is too big I don't know maybe we're too small for so much love maybe it doesn't fit in us and that's why I'm sure you want this too you want this separation you must agree that we need to be apart to give ourselves a chance to heal and to be happy even if it means not being together even if it means we can't live out our love.

You gave me a sarcastic smile. It was evident that you weren't going to hand me on a platter what was entirely yours. You'd never admit defeat. You didn't say a word. You just tore off my shirt and shoved me back onto the sofa, forcing me to lie down. You yanked off my underwear and rammed your finger into my dry vagina. My face was a picture of horror. My body was incapable of movement. I was drained and you knew it. You took advantage of it. You pulled down your boxers and, right there, on the sofa where previously we had made love, you lay on top of me. I let you do as you wished, as if blaming myself for what I had just said. I was dry, and not even your saliva made a difference. You delighted in my pain, and asked: Isn't it good? I didn't answer. Isn't it good? you insisted. I stayed silent. Isn't it good?

No, I said finally. Then, as if to stifle my reply, you pulled out and rammed yourself into my mouth with violence until you came. I could barely breathe. You only withdrew when you were sure I had swallowed everything. Then you held my face tightly and, eyes overflowing with irony, said: See how happy we can be together?

~

We had been together for four days when he asked me: So, why are you here? It was morning and we had just had breakfast. A little while earlier, I had gone out to buy bread and Portuguese sweets (bread pudding, custard tarts, assorted pastries: I like them so much that I'm even capable of devouring them in the morning). I got up from the table and lay on the sofa to answer his question. Playing with my curls, I told him everything: about my paralysis, my sick body, the key my grandfather had given me. I told him I had been to Turkey and that now I was in Portugal looking for my past. I told him that I needed to settle accounts for previous generations, settle my own accounts.

Did you know I was born here in Lisbon?

No way! Really, or are you kidding?

Really, I said with a smile. I was born in January 1979 and went to Brazil in September. But I've still got my *lisboeta* accent, can't you tell?

He gave me a funny look and came over to tickle me, cover me in kisses. So you're an *alfacinha*?

Yes, I said, smiling at the nickname for natives of Lisbon. I'm a real 'little lettuce'. I've even got a Portuguese passport. Want to see it? Pass my bag, please. I showed it to him. See?

He flicked through it, found my hideous photo, and read out loud. Place of birth: São Domingos de Benfica, Lisbon. So it's true, he said.

Yes, I answered, but now let me finish telling the story. You asked, now listen.

I told him about my trip to Turkey, the people I'd met, the house that wasn't there anymore. I told him I'd gone in an effort to get out of the rut I was in, because for a long time I hadn't been able to get out of bed, back in Brazil. I told him about my mother's death, the pain, the mourning. I told him that I still speak to her. I speak to the dead, I said. To the dead who are with me. And then I told him: I once loved a man, and he killed me. I told him about the violence, how he had cut me, and I showed him all the marks, scars. And I said: If that's love, I prefer not to love. Then he lay down next to me on the sofa and hugged me, and we lay there together, squashed into a space that was smaller than the sum of our bodies. And, playing with my curls, he said: No, that's not love. Don't be afraid.

You must have been asleep for a few hours. I listened to you snoring, which gave me the courage to do what could wait no longer. My body shook, but my heart was steady. I got out of bed, taking care not to wake you. I went to the kitchen, and when I got back you were facing the other way. I was afraid you might have woken up. I whispered your name, but you didn't answer.

I approached you and thought how handsome you were as you slept. Your naked body curled around itself gave me a serenity that your waking body didn't. You were white, white, and your hair was a light down on your soft skin. Your hands looked like baby's hands, and suddenly I felt an enormous desire to hold them, but I was afraid you'd wake up. I had spent many days wondering if what I felt for you was love. Looking at your body on the bed I thought that the answer was yes, that what I felt for you was a love of sorts. And it was with this feeling that I gently rolled you onto your back. You grunted something incomprehensible and then sank back into a deep sleep. I stretched out your arms and legs. I stroked your face lightly and touched my lips to yours. I whispered your name again, but you didn't answer. I felt a certainty that I never had before, and my body stopped shaking. I took the two tips of the sheet bunched up at the foot of the bed and pulled it over you, covering you entirely, like a burial shroud. Then I took the knife that I had gone to fetch in the kitchen and, holding it with both hands, ran it through your belly. I felt the metal tear your soft skin, perforate your flesh, your stomach. I felt the metal scrape your ribs, and then I let it go. You cried out with pain and lifted your head, and the top of the sheet slid down. Your eyes were open. Our eyes met for the last time, and that was when I saw rage, fear, and defeat stamped across your face. Then I saw your head drop to one side, and your eyes closed forever. I glanced about and took in the entire room; I saw all the objects that had once been ours. In the middle of the image, our bed. On the left side of the bed, your white body covered with a white sheet. In the middle of your body, the knife with which I had torn into you. In the middle of your body, the sheet was red. And the red gave me even more resolve, assured me that there was no other possible end to our story.

If you don't mind, I'd rather not take you to the airport.

Why not? Don't you like goodbyes either, is that it?

I hate goodbyes, he said. I prefer to hold on to the memory of our time here, knowing that we'll see each other again.

Do you think we will?

His smile was confident when he said: Of course, you'll see.

Okay then, don't take me, but will you stay with me until I have to go?

He answered me with a long hug. The prospect of another parting was making me anxious. I had come to Portugal to undo old ties and had ended up making new ones, and now I'd have to say goodbye again. Although he was sure we'd see each other again, I tried not to think about the plane that awaited me.

I'd like to live in Rio one day, he said.

And I, in Lisbon. Shall we swap houses? We laughed.

But we could also coincide a little too, couldn't we?

Yes, of course, I said. Have you still got a bottle of Alentejo wine?

I do.

Would you like some?

Yes.

We could have a bottle before I have to go to the airport, no?

He came back with two bottles. He opened one and held out the other, saying: Here, open this in Brazil and think of me when you drink it.

Thank you, I said. You're so sweet.

You're the one who's sweet.

And we started joking: my sweetie pie. My coconut custard. My egg tart. My cupcake. Until we found ourselves without clothes on, by which time we had stopped talking. We both had the same playfulness and the same light-heartedness: not in words, but in gestures. We made love as if it were a game, always inventing new things, delighting in each touch — of our hands, tongues, hair, skin, eyelashes. There was something special when we were together. Perhaps it was this childish light-heartedness: we could be children without fear, we could be children no matter what our age. And that was what we did in our last hours together. We drank both bottles of wine (now how am I going to remember you in Brazil?) until, reluctantly, I had to say: I think we'd better call a taxi or I'll miss my plane. Then we grew serious, as he looked for the phone number and I got dressed.

Fifteen minutes, he said.

I screwed up my nose. Why so quick?

Because services in Portugal work, he chuckled.

There was just enough time for me to finish dressing, get my bags, and give him a tight hug and a few passionate kisses. And to stroke his face a few times. And to look into his green eyes and feel mine sting. And to say: I'm really fond of you. And to hear: I'm really fond of you too. And to feel his hands in my hair, playing with my curls. And to say: goodbye, see you; see you soon.

We gazed at each other until the taxi pulled away, even after the taxi had pulled away. My heart was full of joy, but also a little sadness. I kept thinking: When it's all good, why don't things work out? And then I answered myself: Stop thinking like that. It was good and it did work out. I sat there flitting back and forth between positive and negative thoughts for a while. Until I remembered something that a friend of mine always used to say: Love isn't to be kept to yourself, it's to be spread around. When I'd tell him my stories, he'd always say: But you're not a one-love woman, you have to love many times, spread your capacity for love around. I knew that if I told him this story he'd say: Didn't I tell you? Just think: now there's a little of your love in Lisbon, in yet another city. And a city that is so special to you. While my mind was awhirl with all these thoughts, I heard my mobile beep to indicate a new message. On the subject line, his name, and beneath it, the text: *I think I have all the tenderness in the world in my heart. Thank you for existing. Kisses.*

And that is how I was able to leave in peace, to return to Brazil knowing that my relationship to Portugal was no longer a relationship to the past, or from the past.

My grandfather walks into the room complaining about the acrid smell and asking if I am ready for the trip. A serene light streams through the slats in the shutters, announcing that the sun is about to set. I think that another day is ending and that days ending all seem like one single day. I look around me, as my grandfather talks and waits for a response, and I tell myself in silence that I need to put the blanket in the wash, pick my clothes up off the floor, and clean the mould off the walls. I am disgusted at my own cocoon.

He insists, asking if I am ready or not. I wave him over and he sits beside me, hesitantly. I see how much he has aged and for the first time it strikes me that there is no difference between his face and hands — they are all the same withered skin. Without getting up, I take the little box from the nightstand. In it, amid dust, old tickets, coins, and earrings, lies the key. He glances over and sees what I see. He looks at me, and I don't need to say a thing. I take the key, blow the deep layer of dust off it, and reach out to take his hand. I squeeze it tightly and we sit there with our sweaty hands clasped together, the key in the middle, sealing and separating our stories.

Translator’s note

This translation is based on the author’s revised edition of the text, published by Edições BestBolso, Rio de Janeiro, 2013. The author further revised and edited the text prior to its publication in translation.